Life as a Leb-neh Lover

The Identity Crisis of a Maybe-Lebanese

Published by:

Turning Point Books

15th Floor, Concorde Building, Dunan Street
Verdun, Beirut, Lebanon
P.O. Box: 14-6613
Tel: 00961 1 752 100

www.tpbooksonline.com

First edition: March 2011

Text: Kathy Shalhoub
Illustration: Maya Fidawi
Layout and graphic design: Sinan Hallak
Editing: Dina Dabbous

Events, characters, and places in this book are based loosely on real
incidents in the author's life, but there are exceptions where people and/
or events have been fictionalised and adapted in the name of poetic
license and/or for dramatic effect.

ISBN 978-9953-0-1928-4

Printing:
⊙dots

Kathy Shalhoub

Kathy Shalhoub was born in Lebanon in 1978 to a Lebanese mother and Polish father, but by her own admission, she is truly a Lebanese *madame*. At 17 she left Lebanon for New York where she did what all good Lebanese do: she became a *mhandis* (that's an engineer but she also waited tables. The scandal!). Later she moved to Boston to party and possibly get a Master's Degree at the world's nerdiest university, MIT.

Many travels, jobs and relocations later, she found herself in the South of France getting a PhD in Ocean Science. Soon after, she married her three Nevers: - a Lebanese-American smoker.

She's currently living in Dubai where she is completely ignoring 10 years of education. Apparently no one in Dubai is desperate for a specialist in underwater robotics and marine optics. *Life as a Leb-neh Lover* is Kathy's first book but she intends to write many more, none about engineering.

Maya Fidawi

Maya Fidawi, studied painting and sculpting at the Lebanese University's faculty of art. She has since worked on scores of book projects and is a dab hand when it comes to illustration. Maya's debut work with Turning Point in the *Life's Like That* series produced her signature witty depictions of the Lebanese. She seeks humor in her work and professes a passion for making people smile or laugh, whether by conversation or illustration. She lives in Beirut with her beloved husband Ghassan, and her 2 little precious ones, Karim and Salma.

Foreword

When I was 22 years old, there was nothing I wanted more than to leave Lebanon. Having seen first hand the ravages of war, my sole wish was to move to the U.S. - Land of opportunity, freedom, human rights and the 'American Dream.'

My wish came true when Ted Turner offered me a job at his Cable News Network. At 24 years of age, I settled down in Atlanta right in time for the first Gulf War! The following twenty years saw me get married, have two beautiful daughters and move up the ladder at CNN starting as a news desk editor coordinating coverage of the Iraq war to chief editor of Middle East coverage with a myriad of exciting award-winning positions in between. What lies beneath the glossy headlines is invisible to most: The sweat of hard work, the tears of longing for home, the despair of being uprooted from family and friends.

In my early Lebanon memories a young bright girl resides. I admired Kathy's intelligent curiosity and always imagined that she would turn into a successful woman no matter what she chooses to do in life. I also admired how beautiful she was inside and out: A mixture of Polish features from her dad's side and Lebanese qualities from her mom's side and the best education any Lebanese kid would dream of. In my mind I pictured Kathy zipping through life picking and choosing what she likes, when she likes, any which way she likes it.

Then, I read the book and met the woman Kathy has grown to be. She honestly and generously shares with her readers a life filled with choices, challenges and quests. Kathy takes us on her journey of self-exploration where page after page we're reminded that things are not always what they seem. Kathy's glossy headlines are also built on much intensity.

Although our paths have been different, I found myself in so many of Kathy's stories. I laughed in places, fought tears in others, but throughout the book I truly enjoyed the innocence of Kathy's discourse. I hope that you read this book to find the common thread that ties us all together – our imperfection!

Octavia Nasr
Atlanta, Georgia, USA
January 27, 2011

*To Little Zayne, who gave me the perfect excuse to sit down
and do nothing but write.
To Tessa the cat, my longest standing relationship.*

1. Get Me Out of Here!

ʃ ʃ ʃ

An Absurd Suggestion

I'm a fresh 16 year-old and big brother is coming home for the Christmas of 1994.

He left during the civil war when I was 11 and I haven't seen him since. Do I even know this guy anymore?!

For the last 5 years he's been in New York, first studying, and now working. Can you tell that the home-coming is going to be BIG?

Mom has been cooking for practically 2 days non-stop in preparation for the *waleemeh*[1] she's setting out for the return of her eldest son, the only lucky one of us to have an American passport.

The entire family (minus the cats) heads to Beirut airport and he's welcomed with many open arms, a lot of crying, and a machine-gunfire of questions about life in the great USA.

At home, all the relatives we've ever crossed paths with are present, right down to the cousin of the sister of the wife of the uncle. Dinner lasts for a modest four hours before everyone reluctantly leaves.

My brother, exhausted from the flight, the exuberant reception and the endless questioning, steps out onto the balcony for some fresh air and some peace and quiet.

I shyly follow to keep him company. After all, he's my role model. I started playing basketball and got a pet dog because of him (although my insane mutt was nothing close to his Lassie-style German Shepherd).

"So, how are things going?" he asks.

"They're ok... I'm doing better at school, and I'm playing

> **"The only lucky one of us to have an American passport."**

---

1 Feast

basketball now."

"Word? Have you thought about university yet?"

Thought about university? I'm 16! All I can think about is cute boys, what is he talking about?! "Uh, not really… it's a bit early isn't it? I mean I just started Secondary I, I have two years to go after this!" I think that's evasive enough.

"Well, if you want to go to the U.S. it's not really early. You have a lot of preparation tests to take and you have to get good grades in school too."

"What do you mean go to the U.S.? I don't have an American passport."

"You don't really need one you know. You can get a visa on your Polish passport if the university accepts you. You can go to my university and that way you'll be close by if you need anything. You don't even have to do *Bac[1] II* if you go in as a Freshman."

'' I don't have an American passport. ''

My world is turned upside down in an instant. With those few sentences my brother has grabbed the table of my life and flipped it over, strewing all my random existence so far onto the floor.

My mind picks through the scattered thoughts. I hadn't even thought about college up until now. I had never even considered going to America. Plus skipping the torturous Bac II?! Was that really a possibility?! I couldn't begin to imagine!

A kick in the *Rass[2]*

For my entire year as a 16 year-old the thought of going to America had brewed in my mind. My brother's words rang in my ear… "good grades… New York… skip *Bac II*…" I was instantly caught on a hook and couldn't get free.

Was it really possible? Could little me really make it to America?! Little me who had changed school 5 times, been thrown out of one for bad behavior and failed *Brevet[3]* the first

---

1 Lebanese system of education, follows the Baccalaureate model whether French or Lebanese versions

2 Head

3 Government Exams at 10th grade

time around?!

Little me who used to get 12/100 in Math class and didn't remember a thing from History and Geography? Little me who had never had a passing grade in Arabic because my dad was Polish, my Lebanese mom was raised in Jamaica and the only language we spoke at home was English (except with *Teta[1]*!)?

I was so bad in Arabic that during *Qira2a[2]*, the entire class including the teacher would cringe when it was my turn to read. They would brace themselves for 5 minutes of complete agony as I stumbled over the incomprehensible words of a single sentence before the teacher would abruptly ask the next student to read and the class would collectively sigh in relief.

School was deadly boring, I couldn't bring myself to pay attention. Did I really care who the Cavaliers were wooing, what *Abou Nawwas*' poetry really meant and where the difference lay between a compound and a molecule? I didn't. I couldn't. My life was being lived but I was absent. I had no objective and no motivation. I played basketball, I talked about boys with girlfriends, I had my own set of house keys, and my own dog. I felt plenty grown up already so who needed more?

Where on earth was I going? No clue and I didn't care. BUT! Could I actually get grades that were good enough for college, giving myself the opportunity to leave Lebanon, study in America and explore the world? It was a challenge. A big one!

If there's one thing that motivates me it's a challenge. The sudden existence of a remote possibility for escape to something new kick-started me into study mode. Suddenly I cared about school, I wanted to understand magnetic fields and know more about Milton. My grades started inching upwards, my Math and Physics scores sky-rocketed and I was even memorizing my history and geography in Arabic (that didn't mean I understood it!).

I had something to look forward to! I had a goal!

> "Where on earth was I going?"

---

1 Grandma
2 Reading

Mom's on Board

I wasn't sure how mom was going to take the news that her daughter wanted to go study in the U.S.... We hadn't talked about this before, I hadn't mentioned university in the past, I was highly accident prone and a well known cry baby (who gets nicknamed Screama Ballerina?!). I wasn't sure if she could see me flying to the U.S. and navigating American college life by myself.

After preparing a rock solid pitch and launching it to her one night when she had had a couple glasses of Rosé, I awaited her reaction breathlessly.

"You really want to go?"

Was this a trick question? Of course I really wanted to go! "Yes! I really do!" I shrieked. "It would be fantastic mom! A great opportunity!"

"Hmmmm... do you know what you want to study?"

"Uh I'm not sure yet but I'd love to do Marine Biology or something to do with the ocean. But I'm getting really good at Physics at school now so I don't know... And they said in the brochure that I could decide after the first year of electives!"

"Hmmmm..." she said again. I could see that she was mentally weighing pros and cons in her mind. My daughter, America, a good education, her brother is there, the alternatives to leaving... Then she got this distant look in her eyes...

She must have been remembering a moment very much like this in her own past. She had desperately wanted to go to the UK to be a neurosurgeon but instead was 'strongly encouraged' by her parents to stay in Lebanon and study something more feminine (like English Literature...).

I could tell that she didn't want to do the same thing to me. She wanted me to live the life I wanted as opposed to a life she wanted for me. Growing up I had never heard the words 'you can't' or 'because you're a girl' in our house. Not a single time. Why would she start her double standards now?

Mom surprised the pants off of me when she said: "OK. You're going. I'll get you there no matter what it takes!"

I jumped up and hugged her for an eternity. My mom rocked!

"I'll get you there no matter what it takes!"

The Lebanese Dream

By the time I got to Secondary II *(Bac I)*, I was aiming single-mindedly for college abroad. I had somehow metamorphosed from an indifferent delinquent to a brainy, motivated and well balanced 17 year-old. I had a steady boyfriend (who heard that I was leaving about 100 times a day!), I comfortably passed the TOEFL and SAT exams and I studied religiously. When my brother sent me brochures and pamphlets from the university he had been to, I read them repeatedly from cover to cover, committing every word to memory. I filled out pages of applications and waited anxiously for months to get a reply. Every day I hoped I would get accepted and every day I was terrified that I wouldn't.

By April, I received my first official letter from the U.S. that I was accepted at the State University of New York in Stony Brook, Long Island. I must have screamed for 20 minutes before remembering to breathe!

"I must have screamed for 20 minutes before remembering to breathe!"

In May I started working on my visa. Every ounce of my energy was focused on my leaving. Somehow I was ranked second in class for the first time in my life! I sailed through the English and Arabic *Bac I* government exams, scoring the highest grade in Arabic! Take that *ya istez el 3arabi*[1]!

I plodded through one procedure after another. Get I-20[2] from University: Check. Get school transcripts: Check. Get Diploma: Check! Schedule university orientation: Check! Decide on major and classes: uh… later! Let's get the visa first.

Ah, the American visa. Every Lebanese person's dream. Our supposed ticket to freedom. One of the most cherished and revered pieces of documentation a person can hope for! How to get one, now that I've come so far? The American embassy in Lebanon was closed, they were bizarrely scared of being bombed again or something… It was either Syria or Cyprus. For Syria I would need to go twice, once to make an appointment and once to be present at the previously made appointment. Time frame? Fifteen to 30 days. Those were days I didn't have! I had orientation to get to people! Cyprus it was.

---

1 Arabic teacher
2 Form issued by American university to get a student visa

But wait! I forgot that I needed to get back into Lebanon after Cyprus. First, I needed to be Lebanese. Being born to a Lebanese mother and having spent a lifetime here was not enough for the Lebanese government apparently. Through some rare opportunity (that included my parents being separated), we were allowed to apply for citizenship but my nationality papers were in the works and my residence permit had expired.

I applied for a Lebanese visa and got it (I've lived here all my life! Do I really need to apply for a visa?!). Then mom and I headed off to Cyprus. We arrived in Nicosia at midnight on a Thursday. We had an early Friday morning appointment. By 7:00am we were at the embassy with 28 people ahead of us already. The doors opened at 8:35am and were closed by 9:15am with claims of a computer breakdown to shut us up. The first 20 people were allowed in, the rest of us were told to go home. Who cares if you have a flight to catch, orientation to go to, and a life in the U.S. all planned out?! I was crushed. My mom was furious. Wait till Monday they said.

After a long and eventful weekend that included bicycles, a lost wallet, food poisoning and a pool, we were back at the embassy at 5:30am Monday morning. We were number 21. Again we didn't get in. This time, no lame excuse was given. Mom was in a rage! She had work to get back to, we were paying penalties on flights, and my ticket to the U.S. was booked for Wednesday!

We decided to camp out in front of the embassy that night. We HAD to get in the next day! We had planned to be there by 10pm but as we passed by in the late afternoon, we realized we were not the only people with this bright idea. Four others had thought the same thing but beaten us to it. I stood in line as number 5 while mom went to get blankets, a thermos and the papers needed. We spent the whole cold and uncomfortable night there, not sleeping, but not quite awake.

I finally got in the next day, and to my horror, was charged an additional $120 for getting the visa on my Polish passport. They said it would have been $40 on a Lebanese passport. Thanks *Libnen!* We returned that afternoon for the visa but had to miss our flight. My flight to the U.S. had to be rescheduled,

I've lived here all my life! Do I really need to apply for a visa?!

but it was all ok. I had jumped the last excruciating hurdle, and that was it, I was going to *AMREEKAAAA!!!!!*

I'm leaving on a jet plane...

I arrive at Beirut airport 3 hours before my flight. The place is in complete chaos and cars are parked left and right and all over the place. Inside, passengers give their loved ones hugs, and cry their last good-byes before reluctantly detaching themselves from each other and waving until the plane is swallowed into the city smog.

I am there with my own entourage: family, cousins and high-school boyfriend. They are all so sad to see me leave, tears well up in their eyes and warnings to *be careful, please call when you get there…* pour from their lips.

Me? I am so damn excited to get the hell out of here, it's hard to hide it. Here I am, a young girl from next to nowhere, Lebanon, a couple of months short of 18 and on my way to university in Long Island, New York, all by my little self! I feel so grown up and I can't wait to see what's out there! I can't wait for the adventure to start! Finally, for the first time in my life I'm leaving little Lebanon, and heading for the 'land of the free', as seen on TV.

I'm finally following in the footsteps of thousands of Lebanese before me! I'm doing what all my ancestors have done, what the Phoenicians did, what every Lebanese hopes and aspires to do someday: I'm leaving.

On the plane, a young Lebanese couple is sitting next to me. When I open the overhead compartment to squeeze my backpack in, the guy tells me: 'watch out for the cooler please.' The cooler? What, is he transporting his kidney with him or something? He sees the look on my face and knows I'm wondering what's inside. I don't ask anything but he suddenly launches into a monologue like he's just been waiting for the right moment to cry his woes to someone.

'You know, they do this every time I go to visit!', he volunteers, 'I end up leaving with 10 additional kilos of food. You know what we have with us this time?!' He counts off

> **"I'm finally following in the footsteps of thousands of Lebanese before me!"**

the list on his fingers, 'The family is so generous we have 5 kilos of *Labneh[1]* in a cooler. We also have a small pot of *Mehsheh Kousa[2]* , *Kaak[3]* , homemade jam, nuts, *Arak[4]*, a small tray of *Kibbeh[5]* and a few kilos of *Helou[6]*. Every one of my aunts has made me something! There's no refusing them!' He sighs in frustration but his wife rolls her eyes at him... Yum, Labneh! I think to myself and take my seat.

When I finally arrive at JFK airport, I'm speechless. It's an organized madhouse! Giant black women are screaming directions at passengers, Indian (from India) security personnel are fiercely checking our paperwork and Latino immigration officers grill us at the immigration desk. The aggressiveness of people here is as surprising as the variety of nationalities.

At the luggage belt, a young American, obviously aggravated with his trip so far, is standing close by waiting for his bag. An older Indian woman, short, fat, and dressed in full traditional Sari, squeezes in behind him, bumping her trolley into the backs of his legs. He gives her a very dark look. Minutes later she bumps him again in her eagerness to find her luggage. His look gets dirtier. After a few more minutes, another accidental bump.

He whips around furiously and kicks her luggage cart backwards. She is stunned for a second then erupts into a burst of incomprehensible Hindi, waving both arms at him then at the luggage cart, her belly jiggling beneath the folds of cloth.

"Welcome to New York"

He looks at her and calmly says: 'Yeah, welcome to New York!' and turns back.

Hmmm, I think to myself, welcome indeed...

---

1 Soft white cheese or strained yoghurt
2 Courgettes stuffed with rice and meat
3 Hard cakes
4 Anis-flavored alcohol
5 Meat and crushed wheat dish
6 Traditional pastries

2_Culture Shock

{{{

Where are you from?

Yay! So I'm finally here in the great *Amreeka!* Big brother picked me up from the airport, introduced me to some major landmarks of American suburban life such as Wendy's (for fast food) and K-mart (for everything else), then dropped me off on campus. I'm finally at the State University of New York in Stony Brook, just a leap away from Manhattan!

I attended my all-important orientation and learned very quickly that you can't be Lebanese here. I had dressed 'casually' for the first day: jeans, heels, nice top and makeup. But alas! The campus was huge. I got blisters on my feet from all the walking, administrators looked at my made up face like I had just arrived from the Amazon, and students in flip-flops gave me pity-looks as I wobbled on my blisters. There was an unspoken dress code for campus and I had obviously missed the memo.

I am now on campus a full week before classes start, alone on the second floor of my red-brick dorm building. Life for the next few years looks like it's going to be one long corridor of bedrooms shared between 2 girls, and bathrooms and showers shared between many more girls. Yikes! Should I be excited?

Anyway, I met 2 real American girls today. They were checking out their dorms and I bumped into them in the hallway. They were über-friendly like only Americans can be, a pale blonde and a dark brunette with amazingly long black hair; both wore matching tops, overalls and giant smiles.

'HI!!!' They both gushed at the same time. 'Where are you from?!'

'I'm from Lebanon'. I'm pretty sure they were expecting

' Yikes! Should I be excited? '

the name of another state or a local town.

'Lebanon?!? Where is that, like upstate?!' I think they meant upstate as in 'upstate New York', as in not from a city...

'Lebanon like the country.' They looked at me with zero recognition registering on their faces. I elaborated. 'It's a country on the Mediterranean...' Still nothing. 'Beirut is the capital, we're North of Israel?' Aha! Beirut and Israel lit a vague light in their news-starved minds.

'Oh! MaGod! You mean THE Beirut?! There was war there right?!', the blonde's eyes were wide with amazement.

'Yes, that Beirut and no other!'

'Ohhhhh! Wow!!!! How exotic! And you came all the way from there for college?!' They seemed shocked. They had driven 45 minutes to get here and that was far for them.

'Yup', I said, wondering what exactly was exotic about Beirut. Bullet-holes in buildings?

'Hey, so you know,' the brunette with Asian eyes said, 'my parents are originally like, from El Salvador.' That would be why she looked so unusual. But she was born and raised in New York and had the accent and attitude to prove it.

The blue-eyed blonde chimed in, 'And my dad is Puerto Rican but my mom has like Hungarian in her, so that's why I'm so light.'

'Interesting...' I smiled. Don't they say that the U.S. is the melting pot of the world?

"Do you have like terrorists and war and stuff?"

'So what's it like there? Do you have like terrorists and war and stuff?' The blonde wanted to know.

'Do you guys have like color TV and telephones? You know?' The brunette inquired.

Like? You know? OhMaGod?! Were we speaking the same language? And why was 'like' inserted in every sentence?

I gave them the 'Lebanon 101' talk but I didn't think it was going to be the last time. I think by the end of the year I will have perfected a well rehearsed spiel of what people should know about Lebanon - and then some! - because no one I've met so far has a clue where on earth Lebanon is!

College Life

First day of classes? Here goes!

Breakfast: a banana-nut muffin and Yoohoo! chocolate milk.

Time to get to lecture hall from dorm: 20-minutes speed-walking.

View on my way to class: The baseball team in full uniform running drills while the coach whistles and yells at them every few minutes. They looked exactly like I'd seen on TV, exactly!

Most common student apparel: flip-flops, sports shorts and baseball hats. Applies to guys and girls.

Lecture hall: about 12 giant bi-level auditoriums complete with 3 screens in each room.

Number of students taking chemistry 101: 800 in total.

Teaching aids: 4 teaching assistants per lecture, speakers, microphone and transparencies.

Time needed to walk to next class: 10 minutes.

Next class: Marine sciences.

Other classes taken: Anthropology (seriously, we're getting graded for simply reading about African tribes!), Social Sciences, Math, and Computer Programming.

My graduating class in Lebanon was 11 students small! We studied physics, chemistry and 4 different kinds of math. None of this fluffy social sciences stuff. And sports?! An hour a month was more than enough on our single basketball/football/volleyball court.

This university is ridiculous; it's a city all by itself(!) with 20,000 students and 2,000 faculty on 5km of campus. Each subject has its own compound. Engineering needs an entire block to accommodate all the different types!

We have buses that take us from 'North Campus' to 'South Campus' because it would take about 50 minutes to walk.

Campus facilities include: a university hospital and a student infirmary, a power generation station and a sewage treatment plant, a sports complex that includes 6 hardwood basketball courts, a swimming pool, squash courts, 2 gyms, and countless locker-rooms for various sports teams. Outside we have 4 soccer fields, 2 lacrosse fields, 2 football fields and 4 baseball pitches. We have a student center that has its own

"This university is ridiculous; its a city all by itself(!)"

cinema, restaurant and deli. We even have our own radio station that serves the surrounding town and our very own on-campus train station (only 2 hours to get to Manhattan!).

There are tens of sororities and fraternities, two dozen student clubs and every kind of sports team you can imagine, including rugby, rowing and cheerleading. The university even has its own boats for marine studies.

I tried to find the infirmary today and spent an hour lost, and that's with a map. I can't read maps anyway, it's not like we ever used one (or saw one!) in Lebanon.

I'm overwhelmed. Help!!!

Kilos

I'm fat!!! I just discovered today that I'm fat! I was at the gym playing basketball and when I went to change I figured I'd get on the scale just for fun.

Fun?! I've put on 4 kilos in a few months! When did this happen?!

"Three months later I'm a blobby 64?!"

Let's see, when I left Lebanon I was a sleek 60 kilos, and I felt great! Three months later I'm a blobby 64?! Could it be all those giant-sized cookies (the size of a Frisbee) and death by chocolate brownies (can you imagine the size and weight of a double CD case, full of chocolate chips?)

I recently realized that a carton of chocolate milk has about 600 calories in it! That's an entire meal, before I've even had my bagel and banana!

In my defense, my on-campus food options aren't fantastic... All international students are required to have a meal card, (ya3neh[1] we pay for a semester of meals ahead of time and that's that - you don't use it you lose it!) and you can only use your meal card on campus.

When I head to the food court, my choices are Pizza Hut, Burger King or MSG-filled Chinese food. They even deliver to the dorms in case you're too lazy to come get your fast food yourself.

When I hit the all-you-can-eat lunch halls, I can proceed to the salad bar and choose from enormous cucumbers that taste

---

1 Meaning, that is to say

of tree trunk, watery tomatoes reminiscent of wet sponge, and the famous filler: iceberg lettuce. I can also add beans, canned beetroot, 2 kinds of cheese, bacon bits, nuts and raisins (what garden does this salad come from?!). Otherwise, there are Sloppy Joes, burgers, hot dogs, some anonymous vegetable-like matter, and many kinds of pasta and potato. Don't forget the unlimited soft-serve ice-cream on your way out! Where's the real stuff- *Bouza 3arabi*[1] or Gelato?

If I want to be healthy and buy my own food from the one store on campus, the Deli, these are my options:

- A lot of bagels with funky flavored cream cheese. Strawberry? Chocolate chip? Mocha?! It's cheese people!!! And why is a Jewish breakfast so popular anyway?!

- Ramen noodles in a cup, just add hot water for a high-sodium high-carb zero-nutrition meal!

- A bunch of 'healthy' cereal varieties: Frosted Flakes, Captain Crunch, Fruit Loops, etc… Even the oatmeal is prepackaged into tiny packets and filled with sugar!

- Deli sandwiches - probably the healthiest thing there - turkey, roast beef, ham… you even get to pick the vegetables (lettuce, tomato, onion, pickles!) and the type of bread you want. Yay! But how many times a day can you have a Deli-sandwich really?

- A wall full of assorted candy and chocolate that you can have by the shovel full… Diabetes and obesity anyone?

- And finally, the 'Patisserie': a large assortment of muffins, cinnamon rolls, coffee cakes, brownies, and cookies (baked who knows when) all wrapped in oily cling film and sitting miserably next to the more popular Yodels, Twinkies, and other more fluorescently radio-active 'bakery items' they sell. A Twinkie is so filled with preservatives that this unknown cake-matter stuffed with mysterious cream substance can sit on a shelf for 3 months and nothing will happen to it! Nothing!

So please tell me, HOW CAN I NOT GET FAT??!?!?!!

> **"And why is a Jewish breakfast so popular anyway?!"**

Does Size Matter?

I'm not sure if the phrase 'size doesn't matter' was invented

---

1 Arabic ice-cream

in the U.S. 'The bigger, the better' was definitely invented here. Everything I've seen so far is huge.

I tried to get a coffee at the 7-11 the other night. In a normal world, a 'cup' is actually a fixed unit of measurement that really doesn't change. Here, the 'cup' size for a coffee starts at no less than a double D! And that's small! You can drink half liters and liters of coffee and soda if you want. And if that's still too puny for you, try the 1 Gallon soda (3.8 liters in a giant mug!). Also, there's all you can eat buffets, the supersize burgers, and the buy-one-get-one-free option on junk food (you'll never find: buy a pound of lemons, get one free, for example!).

Again, we're at a restaurant with friends, and I order pasta. My dish arrives and I thought we had ordered food for Ethiopia! My plate could have fed a nation and I'd still have leftovers! No wonder people take doggy bags!

The family car of choice is the fugly (= f****** ugly) minivan. His car of choice: Ford or Chevy pickup; her car of choice: cutesy SUV. Whatever happened to the always cool BMW?!

The supermarkets are giant; the aisles, the cakes, the pizzas, the servings, everything! And that can only mean one thing: the people are giant. I've finally witnessed the fat-fight live, and fat has won with a total knockout!

A woman at the mall was so huge that she needed a cane to help her keep her balance. Her center of gravity was at least 30cm out in front of her somewhere between the hills of fat that were supposed to be her chin, boobs and belly. Her belly was hanging down like a dress just above her knees and wobbled aimlessly from side to side with every step she took. Entering a store she blocked the entire two doors with her body mass, and I couldn't stop staring. My friend bruised my arm trying to get my attention but I couldn't look away. What natural disaster or medical malfunction had caused such an apparition?!

I was riveted like you're riveted looking at the sun. This woman alone was practically responsible single-handedly for a solar eclipse! How can size not matter, people?!

> "The family car of choice is the fugly minivan."

Autopilot

As someone who grew up in Lebanon during the war (translation: *bil fawda* or in total chaos), it's taken me some time to adjust to the extreme order that regulates the daily lives of Americans. Everyone stands in a well organized straight line, leaving just the right amount of personal space around each person and politely waiting their turn, asking very few questions when there are hold-ups and remaining impressively calm in the face of long delays. And the lines to get things done are everywhere, sandwich shop, bursar's office, Immigration, banks, supermarkets, movies… you get the picture.

If I'm honest, after some time to adjust, I'm starting to really appreciate not having to fight my way through a crowd any time I need to get something done, not smelling stinky armpits stuffed up my nose as someone reaches over me to get service first, having more personal space than a jelly fish (i.e. not getting boobs and butts rubbing against me as people try to stand as close as possible to their destination), and eventually getting served by a fairly polite person on the other side of the counter who is not being hollered and jeered at by every bully who thinks they are so important they should be allowed to skip the line. I've gotten pretty used to it, and in fact, I really really like it! Who wouldn't?!

But things can always be taken to an extreme. I am beginning to get the feeling that people here have gotten so used to this automated way of life that they fly on autopilot ALL THE TIME!

For example:

Driving is a piece of cake in Long Island. There are road rules, clear traffic lines, speed limits and cops that are meant to keep the order; and order is kept very well, so that eventually you can really relax while driving and not have to be on the defensive all the time.

I was driving to the supermarket today, and I got to an intersection, where, uh-oh!, the traffic light wasn't working. Usually when this happens the light automatically starts flashing yellow: i.e. proceed with caution. This particular light was not. There was a line of 6 cars just stopped there, where

> "Driving is a piece of cake in Long Island."

the light should be, not sure what to do.

I waited for a few minutes (three is a few, right?!) wondering if there was a traffic cop sorting things out, if the leader was going to take the initiative and go since there were no other cars in the intersection, and I generally tried to be a polite and patient citizen. I think given the time I've spent here so far, 5 minutes really was the limit.

Suddenly my Lebanese upbringing kicked in, and I decided that I was quite capable of thinking for myself, and did I really need to wait for a traffic light to tell me how to cross an intersection safely?!

I pulled out to the left of the line of cars onto the extremely spacious and unused shoulder, paused at the intersection to make sure it was safe, and after crossing, was happily on my way to the supermarket. I glanced in my rearview mirror, and one other person had followed my lead. The others were waiting patiently at the broken light, for what, I'm really not sure!

3. Don't They Know Anything?!

ʃ ʃ ʃ

George

People here are still getting used to me and where I'm from.

I met a Long Island girl the other day. She's never left Long Island. This was our conversation:

LI-girl: 'You're from all the way there?! Oh! My! God!'

Me: 'Thanks!'

LI-girl: 'So tell me more! What's life there like? It must be really hard hunh! Do you have cars?' (In other words: Do you eat off the floor, do you have radios, do you play with your feet?)

I'm getting really tired of all this bullshit about how backward we Arab Bedouins are. Also, I thought, surely she knows something … I mean I did get on a plane and fly to New York after all, right?!

Me (sarcastically): 'No. We all ride around on camels.' My sarcasm eludes her and she believes me! So I decide to see how far I can take it. She is wide-eyed and innocent and super-impressed.

Me: 'Yup, definitely camels. We had to ride our camels to school because the oasis where the elders taught us was so far away. And we would have races to break up the monotony of the ride. I had my own camel named George. His mother was a white camel, but George was special because he was a rare Pinto camel and I was the only one in the village with one. I miss him.' Then I looked really sad.

LI-girl: 'Oh my gosh! Where's George now?!'

Me: 'Oh, he died. He got really old…'

LI-girl: 'Oh that's so sad!' Her eyes got watery and she looked like she was going to cry. I felt terrible! I couldn't tell

"We all ride around on camels."

her that Pinto camels didn't exist and that I was joking now!
So much for sarcasm...

You MUST Be Mistaken!

Mrs. M. from the foreign student office calls me for an appointment. There are things in my application that need to be 'clarified'. I'm not sure what she means since I've made the effort to read the questions carefully, write my answers in clear capital letters, and look over the entire application a couple of times.

I arrive at her office and her secretary announces me, trying to pronounce first my last name: 'Miss New-aaaaaa......euhh.... ', then my first name, 'Miss Ka-tarr-euhhh....', and she looks at me in desperation.

I've been here before. 'Ka-ta-gee-na', then I rescue her with a few more words, 'you can call me Kat'.

Mrs. M.: Waves my application in her hand and tells me to sit, speaking in slow careful English so I'm sure to understand.

Mrs. M.: 'So Kat, right? In the section where it says nationality, you have written down here: Polish. Is that right?'

Me: 'Yes, that's right.'

Mrs. M.: 'And under place of birth, you've listed Lebanon - you understand that this question means where you were born, right?'

Me (smiling a bit because I'm starting to see where this is going): 'Yes, I was born in Lebanon, my mom is Lebanese. I grew up there actually'.

Mrs. M. nods in pretended understanding: 'Ok then, you've marked down Nicosia as the place where your visa was issued- your visa was issued in Cyprus?!' She looks incredulous and waits for another explanation.

Me (obliging): 'Well yes, the American embassy in Lebanon is closed ever since it was bombed.' I don't know why I take a perverse pleasure in seeing the horrified faces of Americans when I speak so nonchalantly about bombing and war.

Mrs. M. winces, unsure how politically correct her questions are: 'Okayyyy. Well then, in this section here you've listed

English as your first language. You must be mistaken. First language means the language that you are best at, and have grown up speaking, so your native language.'

I smile again because I am so amused by her discomfort: 'I understand that, and yes, English is my first language.' I leave things there, my sentence hanging, her hanging...

She is more uncomfortable because she doesn't understand: 'I see... so you grew up speaking English? It's your strongest language? Your native tongue?' She can't believe it. 'What about Arabic or Polish?'

'Oh I don't speak any Polish.' I smile again and finally explain to her: 'See my mother grew up in Jamaica and my father is Polish, their common language was English so that's all we spoke at home.'

I assume she's going to be happy now that it's all clear but she only whispers a quiet 'OK' and lets me leave. She shakes her head and mumbles something to herself. She's even more perplexed than before we started. We're complicated, us Lebanese.

Credit

'Guys! Could you keep it down please?! I have an 8:10am class tomorrow morning!'

Amy from the room next door is lying on her bed in front of her TV with a huge bag of Doritos resting on her belly. Four others from my floor are sitting in various locations around the room laughing loudly at an Adam Sandler movie they've seen a few times already. It's 3am.

Mike turns around from the mini-refrigerator where he was reaching for another diet coke and asks me, 'Why the hell did you schedule a class that early?! You're being a party pooper!'

'I know, I know, but it's the only time I could fit Physics into my schedule!' They are surprised at how serious I am, and disgusted that I'm taking Physics in the first place...

Amy crunches through another chip before asking: 'How many credits are you taking anyway, Kat? Like a million?'

'No! 21...' I am starting to realize that I sound like a huge

"You're being a party pooper!"

nerd. They're all taking 14 to 16 credits. I had to petition to take over 18 credits; but I had a lot of courses I wanted to take and the cost was the same, so why not take advantage since my family were busting their ass to send me here anyway?!

'You're such a geek!', someone said. 'You need to relax! Chill out!'

'Well excuse me for wanting a decent education!' I half-smile since I was only half joking. I know I sound like such a nerd but I can't help it.

They are all here on loans or grants, or getting reduced tuition for being from New York. As an out-of-stater, I pay double their tuition. I need to get the maximum mileage possible from this education. And maybe earn a scholarship!

I'm really surprised that with all the advantages and benefits American kids have, there aren't more of them in college. I'm surprised they have good opportunities that they don't take advantage of. They drop out of college because they get bored, can't be bothered to study, or are just not interested... I'm shocked!

On the other hand, they're surprised that I'm taking 21 credits and studying so hard to get a degree. They think I'm super smart. They can't really see that for me, a kick-ass education is the best ticket to independence, to making some money, to getting a scholarship for grad school or getting a well-paying job that comes with a work visa... It's a permanent ticket out of Lebanon!

Half and Half

"I have my first real apartment"

I have my first real apartment, yay, but it's tiny! It's in Selden, a white-trash suburb where people drive minivans, and have a lot of junk sitting in their front yards. OK fine, it's not really meant to be an apartment, it's a part of a garage that belongs to a house and they've converted it into a sort-of apartment to make some extra cash from the $400 rent. The bedroom can barely fit a futon, leaving no space for anything else, and the second room fits a desk, a closet, a counter and a refrigerator. The counter has a hot plate on it. The dishes are done in the bathroom sink, since there is no other.

But all this is beside the point. It's mine. All mine! I have no roommates and no shared bathroom, I come and go as I please, I have my first phone number ever and I have the freedom of, let's say it together, MY OWN PLACE! Woohoo!

But I digress, the point of my story is this: I met my landlords today. They're nice enough, the Schmalenbergers… but not so bright, I think.

They were chatting with me today, the usual small talk:

Mrs. Sch…: 'So, going to school hunh, what are you studying?'

Mr. Sch…: 'Oh! Electrical Engineering, what an odd profession for a girl. Our daughter is studying psychology at UConn'.

Me: ' Oh cool. Well I wanted to do Marine Biology, but they only have a minor, not a major. Anyways, I better get back to my homework.'

Mrs. Sch…: 'Wow you have an exotic accent, where are you from?!'

Me: 'Well, I'm half Polish half Lebanese.'

Mr. Sch…: 'Oh, so you're Portuguese then! How nice!'

Me: 'Hunh? What? No,no, I'm from Lebanon! I'm half- … oh never mind'.

I smiled and left.

Who knew that the Phoenicians invented the Portuguese too?!

ʃʃʃ

4_Clueless

ƐƐƐ

Where Are My People?!

I've been really missing home lately. I'm missing the food, the chaos, the people, the traffic, the language, everything! Are there no Lebanese on campus?! I looked through the international student associations; there are Asians and Haitians, Indians and Jamaicans, Iranians and Russians, Jewish clubs and Catholic organizations, but not a single Arabic speaking club, not a hint of Lebanon or the Middle East anywhere, and I'm missing it!

"Could this guy be Lebanese?!"

In class today, the professor was returning our homework when all of a sudden the words 'Rob Kalaf' pulled me out of my sleep-deprived haze. I immediately jumped! Hunh?! Could this guy be Lebanese?! Could his name be 'Khalaf'?! looked to the guy who raised his hand and saw a short dark haired, dark eyed kid (a bit nerdy looking but hey, it is an Analog Circuits class!). I got really excited at the prospect of finding a Lebanese person among the 17,000 on campus!

After class I ran outside after him as he headed off to his next class. He didn't talk to anyone or look at anyone on his way. Maybe he has no friends I thought! I chased him down:

Me: 'Hey! Hey Rob! Can I ask you a question?!

He turned around with a scared look on his face. I guess I did look a bit psycho in my bright-eyed eagerness. 'Yeah?'

Me: 'Uh, are you Lebanese by any chance? I heard the Professor call your name! '

Rob (looking at me like I was a talking bird that fell out of the sky): 'What? No! No I'm not. I'm American.'

OK, I think you need a visual here. Red-faced, blue-eyed European-looking girl, just chased him down and is leaning over him grilling him about being Arab. She's fidgeting like she's on drugs. A little strange for Long Island. What else would he say!?

My face fell. I had such high hopes of finding a Leby to talk to in Arabic! 'Oh, really?! I'm sorry, your name is so Lebanese and you know I'm Lebanese too, I know I don't look it but I am, and I've been here a couple of years already and I haven't met any Lebanese yet so I thought maybe...'. Then I realized I was rambling. I stopped.

Rob: 'YOU're Lebanese?!?' I nodded. The curse of the mixed genes (I'm really happy with my genes, mom, dad, thanks!) He seemed to loosen up. 'Oh, well my dad is Lebanese but I was born here, and I'm American.'

That was the end of the conversation. He refused to be Lebanese, and I was tired of integrating into the college cultural soup. I was looking to identify with someone, to share my culture and be more myself. I've gotten to the point where I ask anyone with a slightly Arabic-sounding name where they're from in attack mode.

Where are my people?!

The Big Apple

My first trip into New York City, into Manhattan, was a nerve wracking experience. I think I'd seen waaay too many movies about muggings, gunshot wounds and crime to be at ease.

My friends and I took a 2-hour train ride one weekend from the on-campus station into Grand Central Station. When we got out, whoa!!! People of every color, shape and size were pushing and shoving to get to the exit. I tightened my handbag around my shoulder, made sure the zipper was closed and the flap was inwards towards me. I was paranoid that I would get pick-pocketed or that someone would just snatch the whole bag from me. I didn't even wear any jewelry because I kept imagining that some guy would tear my earrings out of my ears and keep running.

An old lady was dragging her bag behind her, blocking

pedestrian traffic because she couldn't carry it up the stairs. People just shoved themselves around her and kept going, not even noticing her limp. On pure impulse, I reach for the bag and offered to help her with it. She held the bag tight and just looked at me like I was a total nutcase, like I was insane and trying to steal her belongings. I guess they're not used to a stranger's offer to help in NYC. I asked her again if I could help her. She was exhausted and just nodded her head.

A guy in a suit next to me noticed that I was helping a stranger and was somehow jogged out of his self-centered daze. He half-heartedly reached for the bag in an I-suppose-I-should-help gesture. I told him it was OK. I was already near the top anyway... My friends looked at me strangely.

'What?!' I said, a little defensive.

'Well, you're just strange! Here you are all paranoid about getting mugged, but then you help a total stranger with her bag...'

I guess I could sort of see their point but I couldn't just ignore the poor woman and walk past her could I?

In the city, we had lunch and went for a walk in Central Park. I was terrified that someone would jump out of a bush with a knife and slash me.

My friends once again shook their heads at me. 'You've watched way too much TV. Why are you so scared?! You come from a war zone!'

"You come from a war zone!"

True... Again, I could see their point, but for me war was a different circumstance. I never heard about rapes and murders and shootings in Lebanon (well random street shootings outside of war that is!). I never felt scared walking alone at night. Over here, even out in Long Island in the middle of nowhere a girl was raped on campus despite all-night patrols by campus security.

Was I really being silly to be scared? I definitely feel safer at home!

Roommates

In the two semesters since her arrival, my sister has had 2

roommates, each one more of a jewel than the other.

So you remember all those Mexican soap operas we used to watch in Lebanon? Maria Mercedes, Anna Christina? Rosa, etc… Well, my sister says she doesn't miss them at all because she has her own soap operas going on right there in her dorm room.

" The first roommate was just batshit crazy. "

The first roommate was just batshit crazy. She was Puerto Rican and must have thought she walked right out of a soap opera herself. Within the second week of the semester, she dumped her high-school boyfriend, who came to this university to be with her in the first place. He begged her. He sent her flowers. He called her all the time. He stood outside her door. He phoned her friends. He did everything!

Meanwhile she was going out with 3 different guys. Experimenting, she liked to say!

He eventually got over her, and towards the end of the semester he started seeing another girl. Roommate Nutjob went completely insane. She flipped out. All of a sudden she wanted him back. She'd cry to my sister: 'I love him! Why is he doing this to me? What have I done wrong?! He's so mean! Blah blah blah', and on and on. She would wait for him outside his dorm in a T-shirt in the middle of November and beg him to come back to her. Payback's a bitch! as they say here.

Eventually she dropped out and the next semester Sis had a new roommate, an American this time.

And with this new roommate came new drama, and new odors. And the odors didn't come knocking either; they broke down the door, barged in and ran Sis over!

Stinky and her boyfriend both had some kind of foot fungus that reeked! Worse than the most pungent rotten cheese you've ever smelled! It was so bad that on the nights when she wouldn't beg me to come rescue her, Sis would sleep with the window open, even though it was below freezing in January and February.

Sis thought she could live with the smell and the extreme messiness. But one day she came home and found her towel and shower slippers both wet. Stinky had borrowed my sister's frickin slippers and put them on her cheesy moldy feet! Yuck! Still, she figured she only had a few months to go and the semester would be over. Better not to make a huge scene. Sis politely asked Stinky not to do it again.

Oh, did I mention that Stinky and her boyfriend were having sex and fondling each other with their fungusy feet across the room from where Sis slept? Since when do you have to knock and wait a few seconds before coming into your own room so you don't have to see your roommate's boyfriend's pasty, skinny, white ass over her pasty flabby white ass?!

Anyway, *tafa7 el kayl*[1] when Sis got back one morning at 10:30 after sleeping over at my place and found empty beer bottles and cigarette butts all over the place; Stinky and her boyfriend passed out in one bed and some strange ho sleeping in Sis' bed with her shoes on. There was spilled beer and ash mixed into a disgusting mud all over the carpet. The smell in the room was overpowering. Cigarettes, stale beer and rotting feet. A half-eaten chocolate donut sat on Sis' homework assignment (the one she needed to turn in that day).

Sis flipped out! She went completely A-rab on them! She yelled at them to all get the f**k up and get rid of their mess. She threw the half eaten donut at Stinky and screamed at her to 'clean this shit up!' Her boyfriend and friend literally ran out of the room. She kept saying: 'I'm so sorry! I'm so sorry!'

Sis told her she was going to class and that the room had better be spick and span when she got back. After that they didn't speak much and thankfully the semester was soon over.

I've never been happier to live alone in my own place off campus. And Sis has never been happier to visit!

Restaurant Dynamics

"Did I tell you that I was working in a hole?"

Did I tell you that I was working in a hole?

I don't mean a real hole obviously, I mean a restaurant, a real American Bar & Grill. I need to make extra cash for pocket money and, after trying on-campus jobs (making sandwiches, cashier, night-time dorm security, and infirmary secretary), I've opted for a job that makes a little more money (or so I hoped!); and that would, of course, be waitressing.

---

1 Enough is enough

I get paid less than minimum wage but I expected to make quite a bit more in tips. In NY almost everyone leaves a 15% tip. Unfortunately I work in, as mentioned before, a hole, where the quality of clientele is, let's be honest here, crap! I'm not being mean, here's what I've had to deal with so far:

There's the old man who came in for a steak dinner. When he was done he whipped out a giant bag of quarters. He counted out 17 dollars and 54 cents in change (he had the exact amount! I take it it's not the first time he's had the ribeye steak with mashed potatoes) and then asked for my address on an envelope to mail me my tip. Yeah, right! Sure why don't I give you my house keys too so you can rob me of what little I actually do have! (I've gotten really paranoid living here!)

Then, there's the middle-class couple who came in, pigged out on everything possible on the menu, including several appetizers, steak and lobster dinners and giant deserts and coffee, and just sat there forever waiting for all the waitresses to be in the kitchen at once, then they ran out on the check! I chased them out to the parking lot and yelled something nasty after their crappy 1984 wood-paneled Chrysler minivan. If you can't afford a restaurant stay home losers! Then I had to scream at the manager so I wouldn't have to pay their bill myself.

Oh, and let me tell you about the 'doctor' who came in with his wife and 2 teenage kids, ordered a burger and got his mayonnaise on the side in a little plastic cup. But he didn't want mayo after all so he made a huge scene that included telling his wife to be quiet, calling me an asshole, and announcing to the entire restaurant that he was, of course, 'a doctor'. Most people now believe that this means 'giant jerk'.

> " I hate cigarettes, but it's been so stressful "

The list goes on…. I hate cigarettes, but it's been so stressful I've started smoking a few just to keep calm. The bartender is the local coke dealer, and most waitresses are his buyers. It took me ages to figure out why the girls always had 'colds' and a 'runny nose' … ahem ahem!

The manager is such an ass that the host who seats people spends his spare time putting Visine eye-drops into his coffee to give him the runs, and the head waitress is having an affair with the Mexican cook whose wife keeps popping in to check on her *hombre*, and all the wait-staff steal money when they can.

If you're looking for drama - beyond my sister's domestic soap fest - go no further, you've got it all here, sex, scandal, drugs and theft!

I think I'm going to look for a more respectable job tomorrow. This is ridiculous…

Snow is Falling…

Snow is falling all around me
Children playing having fun
It's the season of love and understanding…
YEAH RIGHT! Not in NY it isn't!

It snowed all night and Sis was sleeping over. We had to get to classes in the morning and my crappy 10-year-old Jetta wouldn't start. Sis and I pushed it out of the driveway hoping that it would start with a push. But did it? No.

Great.

Why did we push in the first place?! I'm a college student living in the suburbs. It's not like I can walk to a bus stop or train station! And forget calling a cab! It'd cost me a month's rent. We tried pushing it down the street because eventually there was a hill that would help, and if not, there was a mechanic at the bottom of the hill.

So there we are, 2 girls pushing at this crappy car in calf-deep snow with people driving past us on the left, honking if they thought we were in the way. Honking! At home we'd have a line of people stopping to help us with a push or offering a ride!

We just figured this was NY and that's how people were here.

A few minutes later no matter how hard we pushed, the car wouldn't go forward anymore. It was stuck in a snow bank in front of someone's house. Damn it!

After a while, a man from the house came out and asked if we needed help. Oh how nice! We both thought, totally relieved. Finally someone with a little decency offering to help!

He came and pushed the car with us until it moved about a meter and a half… We were just starting to get momentum

> At home we'd have a line of people stopping to help us

when he walked away to his car and got in. He warmed up his car and drove off, yelling 'good luck' out of his window as he sped past us.

After a few open-mouthed moments we finally realized that he had only offered to help because we were blocking the exit from his driveway. So much for friendly neighbors and helpful citizens.

Our car stopped on the *Autostrade*[1] in Lebanon once a long time ago. It was me, my mom, and my sister. In 2 minutes there were 3 cars stopped behind us to help, and some dude offered to drive us home. I miss that about Lebanon. I really do!

Snowboarding Birthday

I was snowboarding down an icy hill
My face fully covered from the biting chill
Suddenly I got hit hard from the back
I felt I was under massive attack
I flew in the air and landed on my bum
I tore my shoulder and broke my thumb
The little shit who hit me raced away
Before my burst of insults found their way
My sister thought I might be concussed
She stood over me and made such a fuss
A hot rescue skier came to help
He put me on a stretcher and tightened the belt
He skied down the mountain with me in tow
My view: his muscled ass and flying snow
At the infirmary they told me not to fall asleep
So I chatted with the rescuer, he was a creep
My sister took me home and pampered my shoulder
I guess I should be more careful now that I'm older!

‡ ‡ ‡

1 Highway

5. Grad School Bliss

ʃ ʃ ʃ

Stalkers!

Undergraduate classes were completed and graduation was attended. What next?! A career? A decent paycheck? A stable job? Of course not. Instead, try a dream come true. I'm on scholarship for a Master's in Ocean Engineering at MIT in Boston. Yay!

But ever since I got here I've been stalked by the United Nations of weirdoes. I'm not sure whether to feel flattered or creeped out. Am I a weirdo magnet? Or am I just plain stupid?!

First there was the chubby Chinese guy from my math class. He cornered me outside the dorms at 4 in the morning during a fire alarm, telling me how I was in his math class and asking if we could be friends. Then he sent me an email telling me all about his problems and how I seemed like a nice person and a good listener. When I asked him how he got my email address, he claimed he 'remembered' my name from seeing it on my homework. Now my name isn't Mona Haj or Jane Smith. My Polish name is a total of 21 letters composed mostly of a ridiculous series of consonants that should never be placed behind each other. Bottom line, it's extremely difficult to remember from a glance.

Then there was the Turkish guy. We were just friends (as usual) when he decided that he was moving to California but wanted to have a relationship with me. When I tried to tactfully refuse by saying long distance wouldn't work for me, he said we could have an 'open' relationship, i.e. we're together only when we're together and with someone else when we're apart. Nice hunh?! When I said that would never work for me and I was just not interested, he tried to kiss me by force,

"Now my name isn't Mona Haj or Jane Smith."

whispering the whole time 'let it be, just let it be!' as if I was desperately fighting my emotions of passion for him and was dying to throw myself into his arms like in some TV drama.

After that, the Dutch guy. We played pick-up basketball together a few times. He always stared at me with large goldfish eyes, that bug-eyed unblinking look that creeps you out completely, especially when the guy's eyes are pale. For about a month, every few days I'd open my office door and he'd be just standing out there or wandering the hallways… apparently just 'passing through'. In a building 20 minutes away from his own. Yeah, right!

In my dorm building there's this Haitian guy. We cook together sometimes because the entire floor shares a kitchen and we both happen to be there at the same time. One day he offered to cook me a Haitian meal. I figured we're friends so why not. Meal done, I left the kitchen and went to my room. I'm in my pajamas when suddenly there's a knock on the door; it's the Haitian guy. He looks at me and goes: 'I love your pajamas, will you take them off and give them to me?' Needless to say I slammed the door in his face. I have never heard a worse pick-up line!

> "This guy is at least 55."

Then, in the one fun class I am taking, over at nerd central, scuba-diving, I get stuck with an American love-struck scuba instructor. This is not some 20-something guy, with a muscled tanned swimmer's body in Speedos. This guy is at least 55. He's old. He has white hair and a pot belly, and you NEVER want to see him in Speedos. Clear?! He offered to pick me up from the airport as a favor when I got back from a visit to Lebanon. Awww, I thought, a nice person who is willing to help for a change. I'm an idiot. What I should have thought is: He's a man, *ya hableh!*[1] He picked me up and drove me home, then leaned in with his eyes squeezed shut and a big pucker on his lips. Ewwww!!!!!!! Awkward and icky! I almost ran out of the car. Thanks for the ride and have a nice life!

The list goes on but some things are certain: a) I'm too naïve, b) MIT has many (often socially retarded) weirdoes, c) I need to move off-campus next year, and d) I need to leave this university soon!

---

1 You idiot, silly, fool!

Advisor to the Gods

My thesis advisor is a true gem. In fact, I owe him a debt of gratitude for opening my eyes to the facts of life.

During my interview with him to get accepted, he boasted with such pride that at MIT, they put the pressure on students to the max, and once the students couldn't handle it anymore, they would add a little. He said: "We only select the cream of the crop, and from that cream we only take the top layer. We like to weed out the ones who can't handle the pressure."

A typical PhD advisor has a maximum of 4 students so that he has the time to counsel, supervise and nurture their research careers. My advisor has 20 students. We see him for half an hour per month, only by appointment, and we are required to bring a progress report with us.

In that half hour, do we cover progress we are making and snags we are hitting upon? Does he listen to our issues and provide valuable guidance for the next steps? No. Instead he motivates us by telling us how our generation is worthless, how he came to MIT from China when he was 16, and, years later, he is still there as Dean of the Engineering Department. He instills in us a sense of self-worth by pointing out how far behind him we are already, and he teaches us to aspire for more each time he crows at us that he is the greatest scientist there ever was. How can we not be moved?

'Life is miserable.'

I am moved alright. Moved to tears. I study hard, I take all kinds of math classes and put effort into my research, I spend hours on homework and in the Library, I don't sleep before 3am each night. Life is miserable.

Everyone I know is so proud of me for getting into MIT. My family, my friends, even me! But hey, now that I'm here, I'm beginning to realize a few very important things in life.

Here is my advisor, a 45 year-old man from China, and he has been in the same place doing the same thing with the same people and on the same subject for almost 30 years. The highlight of his life, his pride and joy, is a blue M3 BMW he has finally managed to buy. He boasts about how his daughter is able to do infinite fractions at the tender age of 3. Poor kid.

I look on in horror! Is this my future?! Is this where hard

work gets you? I am spooked. Life is too short to spend it busting my ass for nothing. Whatever happened to living?!

I worked so hard in undergrad to get here, and now what?! I could look forward to a non-life of more hard work and my reward being the 'science'?! Being 'the greatest xyz ever'?!

It's a scary thought but I can't quit now! There's too much pressure. From professors, from family, from friends… from myself! Little me from Lebanon is at MIT!

Macho Man

I was stopped by the world's largest a-hole today. Sis and I were driving along at a cool 70mph on the interstate from New Hampshire to Massachusetts after spending a fantastic-ish weekend snowboarding (more ice anyone?) when we see this New Hampshire cop decked out in full boots, tight pants and forest-ranger hat standing in the middle of the coming and going highway (the wide grassy divider between the two). He was flailing his arms around like he was trying to land a plane on the grass strip.

I look at my speedometer and I'm within the accepted speeding limit (+10 of whatever is posted), plus the guy has no radar with him so I look at Sis:

Me: 'Is he trying to tell me something? Is that for me?'

I'm starting to panic but I'm sure that when I got my license they were very clear about specifying never to pull over on the divider, absolutely NEVER! so I didn't. I kept going and figured he was waving at the car behind me or something.

Less than 5 minutes later the bastard is riding my ass with lights and (can you believe it?!) sirens! WTF? I pull over to the right shoulder like an obedient citizen and stay in the car, rolling down the window. He marches over spewing anger and righteous indignation.

Me: 'What did I do officer?' I'm trying to stop my heart beating out of my chest and to stay calm.

Officer Jackass: 'SHUT YOUR MOUTH AND GET OUT OF THE CAR!' He's obviously hollering.

My sister and I are both shaking but she pats my arm

> " Is he trying to tell me something?"

quickly and whispers 'be nice!' before I get out.

Officer Jackass: 'Hands on the hood!' Before I'm even completely out. I'm not a criminal, what's his problem?!

Officer Jackass: 'Did you not see me back there?!'

Me: 'I did but -'

Officer Jackass: 'Why didn't you pull over?!'

Me: I didn't understand your hand signals and I didn't know you were referring to me! I wasn't speeding!'

Officer Jackass: 'You were speeding and I told you to pull over. You deliberately ignored me!'

Was he neglected as a child perhaps...?! Did his fragile ego get squashed when he was ignored?!

Me: 'I didn't! I have no idea what this means!' I re-enacted his stupid plane-landing signals. I was getting pretty angry at being treated unfairly.

'Plus, it says in the New York driver's manual never to pull over on the divider, I was following the law!'

Officer Jackass: 'I am the law,' he yelled, 'and this is not New York. Your U.S. license is an honor not a privilege! Stay here.' He marched off to his car.

I walked over to my sister.

Sis: 'Don't argue with him. He's an ass, just agree with what he says and let's go!'

She was probably right, but it's so difficult when such a jackass on a power trip is up in your face!

He comes back and hands me 2 tickets.

Officer Jackass: 'You're getting ticketed for speeding (OK...) and a ticket for evading a police officer (what?!)'

Me: 'What?! Why?! I wasn't evading anything -'

Officer Jackass: 'I don't want to hear any arguments.' His little penis was making him totally unreasonable. Fine, I'll play it your way macho man!

I looked down at the tickets for a second and concentrated on feeling sorry for myself. The price on the tickets helped a lot: $150 and $250. The tears started to flow. Suddenly I felt really sorry for me and I started crying for real and talking loudly and hysterically.

Me: 'How do you expect me to pay for this?! I'm a grad student. I make peanuts all year. This is the first vacation I've

"I'm a grad student. I make peanuts all year"

taken in years. I wasn't even speeding. And how am I supposed to understand your hand signals. I'll have to get a second job to pay for this -' I run out of breath.

A macho man is nothing in the face of a woman's tears, I've learned.

Officer Jackass looks at me for a few seconds as I wipe snot from my nose: 'OK OK, give me one of the tickets, just stop'.

Sis threw the more expensive less pleasant 'evading a police officer' ticket in my direction. She's a smart cookie that one.

Officer Not-So-Macho tore it up and gave me a brief don't-do-it-again talk. I wiped my running nose and eyes as Sis wisely thanked him.

I hate cops, especially little cops with large Napoleon complexes!

Falafel Their Way

There are many food trucks outside university buildings in general because the food is cheap, OK-tasting, and students are too lazy/tired/busy to go any further than outside the building for supplies.

There's a falafel truck outside the building I work in. I was quite excited to find out that the owners were Lebanese. And in any case, who can beat a falafel sandwich for two dollars?!

After some hesitation, I finally get the courage one day to go and try one. I wait in line with a variety of Asians, Indians, and Caucasians, none very Arab-looking, but I don't think about it too much.

It's my turn and I ask for a simple falafel sandwich.

The lady asks: 'Lettuce, tomato and mayo with that?'

'Hunh?! What? Excuse me?'

She repeats herself without much enthusiasm.

'Uhh, don't you have taratour[1]? And lifit[2]?!' I'm a bit surprised.

'We have a yogurt sauce' she said.

The 'a yogurt sauce' didn't sound too promising... but I figured it would beat mayo with falafel, right?!

When I left and finally tried my sandwich, it really didn't

> It's my turn and I ask for a simple falafel sandwich.

---

1 Sesame sauce
2 Pickled turnips

taste much of falafel; it tasted more like a veggie burger thrown into a lot of Arabic bread. At least the bread was real.

So much for my dreams of a real *falafel*. It's really just a McFalafel burger and not our beloved *Falafel Sahyoun*[1]!

I Think I'm Schizo

I really am beginning to feel bipolar.

Every time someone asks me where I'm from, I'm so proud to say from Lebanon. When they say it's the land of terrorists and Beirut is nothing but a war zone, I get worked up. I defend Lebanon fiercely, and then proceed to enumerate all the wonderful things about our culture, our people, our language, our food... My conversations sound very one-sided, clichéd and pretty much like a tourism flyer.

A sequel or offshoot of the Lebanon 101 spiel, The Lebanon Hard Sell goes something like this:

- In Lebanon, we have beautiful mountains where you can go skiing (in winter) and then drive down to the beach in 45 minutes. The snow is always fluffy like Spring snow and the sun is out most of the time, so we have fabulous skiing conditions.

- In Lebanon, the beaches in the north and the south are great, so blue and so clean and so wonderful...

- In Lebanon, our food is healthy; we eat a lot of fruit and vegetables, beans, pulses, rice... (the famous chickpea!) And the *labneh*, yum! It's all so healthy! The food is so good! A lot of things have garlic and lemon in them but they're so much better that way! And don't even let me start with the desserts and pastries... (a dreamy expression slides across my face as I start to drool).

- In Lebanon, the nightlife is fantastic! We go out late and the music is always good and the alcohol is affordable and people dance until dawn and have a really great time! The clubs are so original too... (like *BO18*, a club notorious for being built over a mass grave in a macabre underground design that opens up as a coffin, the open lid giving way to a view of the dawn sky!).

---

1 One of Lebanon's widely recognized and most prized falafel vendors near downtown

In Lebanon, etc...

Then during my visits to Lebanon, the first day I'm shocked that this is the paradise I've been touting to people. The highways are a mess, the asphalt is full of potholes, there are random billboards stapled all over the crooked roads and over each other, the buildings are dusty and dirty, the road signs (when you find them) are faded, people drive like maniacs and are aggressive as hell, the public beaches (what public beaches?!) and even overpriced private ones are dirty, and besides who on earth would want to go skiing in the morning then to the beach in the afternoon anyway?

Politeness is a thing of the past, and common courtesy is a myth. Women are shallow and men are shallower, concerned only with driving fancy cars and wearing the latest fashion... Bureaucracy is atrocious, and it takes days and several visits to different government agencies as well as several bribes to get a single document done.

Employees are lazy and unhelpful, and there's general chaos everywhere. We have no electricity, but we pay electric bills, then we pay to have or participate in the cost of a generator and pay for *mazout*[1]. In addition, and because that's so expensive and not always foolproof, we also pay to have a UPS for periods of low power usage. Then we pay water bills to the water company, but we have no water. We have to order bathing water by the truck load and drinking water by the bottle, and because there is no electricity, we have no warm water and no water pressure for the shower anyway.

What is wrong with me?! When I'm in the States, I can't stand it there and Lebanon is wonderful, and when I'm in Lebanon, all I can see are the flaws and limitations of life in this small country. Am I completely schizophrenic? Am I nutso? Half-blind? What's the deal?

Epiphany

I failed my qualifiers.
I was technically in the PhD program, but to actually be on

theres general chaos everywhere. **

---

1 Diesel oil

the list, I had to take qualifying exams that would allow me to continue on the PhD track. After 6 math classes and countless others in mechanics, fluid dynamics, and underwater structures (all passed with a B!), I failed the qualifiers by 2 points.

My advisor was fuming. 'You'll take them again next year!' he commanded. 'You just have to study more. You need to spend every waking hour in the library!'

I thought I already was spending every waking hour in the library?! I had busted my ass studying for these tests, but they were hard, and I can't say I was passionate about my subject. I was just going along for the ride. I was much more interested in real life than in the perfect design of a naval vessel…

Then there's my dad. I had been promising to visit him in Poland ever since my parents separated years ago. He kept telling me how proud he was of me for getting into MIT and told anyone who listened which school his daughter went to. He passed away just before my qualifiers and I never got to see him. On the one hand I was glad I didn't have to explain myself to him, but on the other hand a black hole of regret opened up inside my heart. I felt like a failure not because of the qualifiers, but because I had broken a promise that I would never be able to make up for.

I got to thinking that life at MIT meant exactly that: life at MIT and nowhere else. Being at MIT cancels out your entire existence in the rest of the world. I had just spent 2 years slaving away over math and homework, while the rest of the world revolved around me, hearts continued to beat, lives continued without me, and people lived and breathed and died while I was still doing the same thing. I had lost touch with the real world.

On an impulse, I accepted my friends' invitation to skip school for 2 weeks and hop down first to the Bahamas, then to Brazil for *Carnavale*.

Did I have the money? No. Charge it! Did I have the time? No. F**k it! I had failed anyway. Was I going to sustain endless disapproving smirks from my evil-eyed advisor? Who cares! I needed a breather.

The trip was amazing, it was everything I could never have imagined it to be. People were out there living their lives under the sun, their toes dancing in the sand, their smiles surfing azure waves, and their hearts in an endless samba of love and life…

What was I doing holed up in a cold office memorizing equations and reading about fluid flow?! What kind of life did I have to look forward to? Making money? Being fulfilled by scientific discoveries? Designing a revolutionary ship hull? Booooo!

As the carnival revelers sambaed into the night wearing flamboyant smiles and drunk on life, I had my epiphany. I knew for sure that I was not where I was meant to be. Pressure and disapproval from family and friends be damned. What did 'I' want?!

I got back and told my advisor I would be leaving that year with my Masters instead of continuing. I had found a job with a small company in Cape Cod and I was moving. His face turned bright red. It was an insult to his great advisory skill. 'A Masters is nothing but a consolation prize for a PhD!' he screamed at me.

I was immune. My soul was armor plated with the smells of coconut oil, my heart was dancing in the distance to another samba tune and my mind was already MIA, exploring parts of the world I never knew existed.

6. I'm a Professional Now

ƒƒƒ

Who Needs Vacation?!

Since leaving university behind and officially entering the work-force, that is to say the real world, I have to say that I've been fairly happy with the way things are going. I make money, I have evenings to myself, no homework, no evil advisor, and no late night dates with library desks. But as always, I do have a bone to pick with one issue or another. Here we go!

So, It's looking like once you get into corporate America, the word vacation completely loses its meaning. I am now officially employed in an American company. This means that I get 13 days of proper vacation a year. In case that wasn't clear: THIRTEEN.

"Woo-frickin-hoo!"

Also, as I was happily informed by the secretary (like she was bestowing some great honor on me!), I get another 11 days that are public holidays. Woo-frickin-hoo!

Did you know that you lose an entire day alone flying to Lebanon? And it takes a day to get back: so yay for me, I get to go home for less than two weeks once a year and that's it. The rest of the time, sit and work, you number!

Listen, vacation time is a big issue for me. I'm perfectly happy to sit and work, and to be a hard worker too, but I need some vacation time every few months! There are places in the world I want to visit, and countries I want to travel to (now that I have some money!), but I also want to go home once a year. Not fair!

After some research, I found out that the U.S. federal government dictates that employees are given exactly zero paid holiday and vacation days a year. If you get vacation at all it's because the state you live in says you should get a few days or because the company you work for is giving you 'benefits'! And the weirdest thing is: most countries that give 20 to 40 days of vacation are the most productive countries in the world! Take that corporate America!

I am very lucky at least that my company lets me work as much overtime as I like (lucky?!) in exchange for travel time, so that every extra hour worked is an extra vacation hour earned. What other options do I have?!

It's late at night, and a French colleague and I (did you know they get at least 25 paid working days of vacation a year in France?!) are working to accumulate travel time. After all, we're working to live, we're not living to work!

We're bitching about not having enough vacation time when an American colleague walks in. He's working late but not really accumulating travel time - he has about 7 years of vacation that he hasn't taken.

He hears us whining and goes: 'Hey what are you two bitchin' about?! How many times can you go to the Bahamas anyway?!'

This is a guy who spent his last vacation fishing for a week. And his last vacation was probably 4 years ago…

I'm not a robot! How can I survive on 13 days of vacation and 11 holidays a year?! Take me back to school (maybe not!) or to Europe!

The Card is Green

I was called into the HR office today.

It seems that I'm an idiot.

HR noticed that it's been a while since they got me a work visa for the U.S. and gave me the attached green-card application. The one that I still haven't filled out.

They know that although I'm Lebanese, I have a Polish passport too.

They don't think either passport counts for much.

They want to know why I haven't filled out the green-card application yet.

I said it's because I wasn't interested in American citizenship and planned to leave in a few years.

They roll their eyes and patiently explain to me that with a work visa, I have the right to eventually apply for American citizenship. Then they repeat in case I've gone deaf and stupid: 'A-me-ri-can ci-ti-zen-ship'.

Then I roll my eyes and say, thanks, but no thanks. There are other places I want to live in.

Then the 'buts' start coming:

But you don't understand… but this is a great opportunity for you… but people would kill to be in your position, but but but…

They seem deeply offended, shocked, taken aback that I am giving up the opportunity of a lifetime because I have some silly idea in mind about living in another country?! What country could be better than the great U.S. of A.? I mean really?!

I am surprised that they are so shocked at my desire to leave a country where I am constantly freezing, where the last time I saw sun was three months ago, where I pay through my nose for heating bills, where 30% of my income is gone in taxes, where all the food is either genetically modified, has some sort of corn-syrup in it or is pumped with hormones, where I get 13 days of vacation a year, where people look at me like I'm an exotic bird at a zoo, where dinners start at 6:30 and end at 8, where you can go to war at 18 but you need to be 21 to drink alcohol, where 'fun' means getting shit-faced and passing out in your own throw up, and where a man named Bush is president!

"don't shoot, I'm an American!"

Maybe it's not like that all over the U.S., I wouldn't know, but I certainly don't have the vacation time to find out! I want a better quality of life, a better standard of living as opposed to having the honor of holding a card that's green in my pocket that will let me, maybe one day, say to people: don't shoot, I'm an American!

Hypocrisy

Here's an interesting little travel story.

I was sent to Sicily last week for some work, and was flying back via Milan. My mom and brother were flying to the U.S. from Lebanon for a visit so we arranged to be on the same flight to New York from Milano, and we met at the airport.

I got to the airport at my scheduled time, and after waiting an additional hour and a half for my mom's delayed flight, I finally met up with mom and Bro in the international terminal. This was the easy leg of the flight. Now came the hard part. Check-in to go to the U.S.

My mom, being Lebanese, was loaded down with bags of duty free including several kilos of *Baklawa[1]*, nuts and Cuban cigars (Thank God she left the pots of *mehsheh* and *kibbeh* at home!). I wisely swapped my carry-on with hers.

Surprisingly, the check-in part went fairly smoothly for all 3 of us. Fairly smoothly being only an hour for pre-check-in questioning, check-in interrogation and the post-check-in search. Not bad, I thought to myself optimistically. It was the boarding that took me by surprise.

There we were, in the departure lounge, 3 Lebanese, hovering impatiently near our boarding gate after a too-long layover, waiting for our 'zone' to be called, me weighed down with kilos of Lebanese sweets and innocently disguised Cuban cigars when all of a sudden, a flight attendant walks over to my mom and brother and says: 'You are from Beirut, come with me.' So I start walking with them towards where he pointed and he goes: 'No, not you, only them.'

Well I'm indignant here!

Well I'm indignant here! I want to be discriminated against too! I say, 'Well we're together!' So he says, 'OK come this way. '

We are all shuffled over to the search area behind a black screen where we join a huge red-faced Russian with his yellow shirt flapping at his waist. He looked humiliated. I now understood. This was a random search of all the 'terrorists' flying to the U.S.

I stood silently, weighed down by 250 Cuban cigars and 5 kilos of oriental nuts and sweets in a bag covered with Arabic writing, while my brother and mother got felt up by an aggravated Italian guard. As he finished, I approached to get searched as well but the guard casually waved his arm at me saying: 'No you are coming

---

1 Lebanese pastry, better known as Greek or Turkish Baklava, but we maintain it's Lebanese!

from Italy, no search.'

I admit I appreciated their candid honesty a lot more than the more ubiquitous politically correct reply: this is a random search ma'am!

But damn, how hypocritical has the world become to actually separate flyers depending on their country of origin regardless of what they're carrying? And how far is this idiotic war against terror going to go before we realize that we're just aggravating a lot of people and not getting any closer to a solution?

"What next, DNA screening?"

What next, DNA screening?

7 This is Life?

£ £ £

Time to Partay?

I once swore I would never have a roommate again. This was in grad school while I was doing my Master's. I had one particular roommate who was nasty! Her side of the room was always dirty, she would always come home and strip completely, sit on her bed in front of the fan with her fat blubbery legs wide open, and turn the fan on full blast. She felt that she needed to explain herself. Apparently she had some sort of infection, ahem, down there…

And if that wasn't enough, she once left bananas in a bag under her bed so long that I had to call 'health and safety' to come to our room and find the source of the smell. She had insisted it wasn't from her side, and the smell of rotten organic matter was just too much to bear!

Throw that in with my sister's experiences (Roommates, p. 21) and yes, I did swear NEVER to have a roommate again.

"I did swear NEVER to have a roommate again."

Alas, moving to Cape Cod in summer is not the best time, and finding a place to rent is pretty much impossible. I eventually got so desperate that I rented a 4 bedroom farmhouse and yes, got housemates (a step up from roommates, I dare say)! A couple of nice guys and a 19 year-old Barbie-style air-head. I was clear that there were rules in the house; the kitchen and bathrooms needed to stay ultra clean, and in my freakishly organized way, I made a cleaning schedule for everyone.

Life at the farmhouse was lived in harmony for a while until one weekend Bubble-Head asks me if she can have a party Saturday night. Well I'm 25 but I'm not a party-pooper yet, so I said 'Sure!', I'm all for having fun, 'As long as nothing gets destroyed and the house looks like it does now.'. (I meant clean and intact! I had paid the security deposit myself after all!). I was away for the weekend so I couldn't supervise.

She said, 'Oh, of course!'. So of course it was.

I got back Monday morning at 7am to a total barn! It looked like a tornado had hit the house while I was gone. The screens on the windows were torn, there were 2 beer kegs on the storage room floor, the carpet was soaked with beer (and crappy beer too, Budweiser!), the kitchen and living room floors were all sticky with spilt beer, I found my towels on the floor soaking beer up, the couch was torn, there were broken plates in the kitchen and paper cups all over the lawn outside and there was garbage everywhere. I mean everywhere!

How can I not lose it completely?! I was raised in a home, not in a frickin garbage dump! I stomped up to her room and barged in. She was in bed with her boyfriend. I screamed at her like I've never screamed before!

'WHAT THE HELL IS THIS MESS?! YOU SAID YOU'D CLEAN UP! IS THIS WHAT YOU CALL CLEAN?!' I was in a purple rage.

She jumped up from her sleep and looked at me, her lip trembling. 'We c-c-cleaned y-yesterday...'

'YOU CLEANED? WHAT KIND OF CLEANING IS THIS?! I'M RESPONISBLE FOR THIS HOUSE! GET YOUR ASS UP AND CLEAN THE WHOLE PLACE! AND WHO USED MY TOWELS? AND TORE THE SCREENS? FIX EVERYTHING LIKE IT WAS OR ELSE YOU'RE PAYING FOR ALL THE REPAIRS AND YOU'RE OUT!' I slammed her door as hard as I could and stomped back down the stairs. That afternoon I got back from work and found a giant gift-basket in the kitchen with my name on it. She had new towels in there, candles, soaps, etc... she had a note that said she was sorry. The house was clean enough.

Yesterday she had the nerve to ask me if she could have another party. Did I say yes?! *Akeed la2!*[1] I'm not crazy!

Never again will I live with strangers. For real this time!

'Never again will I live with strangers.'

The Cost of Comfort

Since I've become a bona fide money-making professional,

---

1 Of course not!

my college lifestyle is behind me. This means I can rent a spacious house that's all mine (bye bye roommates!), and eat more fruit and vegetables and buy better quality meat (beef for example as opposed to ground chuck, whatever that is!), and even organic eggs and milk so I stop growing hair in the wrong places (i.e. my chin!) because of all the hormones pumped into the food. So hooray for me.

After my summer roommate drama and my sister's experiences, I've rented a great 3-bedroom house that is right on the water in Cape Cod. No really, if I jump off the back deck I'll be knee deep in sea-water and swan poop. If we were in summer that is. In all 1.5 months of it…

In winter however, I seem to find myself with a lifestyle slightly worse than college. And this is all in my very own 3-bedroom house. I conveniently picked the only year in ages (people tell me) where it snows so much in Cape Cod.

My house is freezing cold despite the heating. The oil heating. The first really cold month of winter, I would turn the heat on when I got home and turn it off before leaving home. My bedroom was warm enough and the rest of the house bearable. This one month alone cost me over 400 dollars!!! And seriously, winter here is essentially 7 months; I'll be broke before I'm warm!

So instead of sleeping comfortably in one of 3 rooms on a giant bed, I have had to resort to turning on the one electric heater in the house, (the one that is BOLTED into the living room floor!), laying my 0 degree F sleeping bag on the floor in front of it with a quilt on top, and camping in my own living room so I can get some semblance of warmth!

In the morning, the first thing I do after the alarm rings for the hundredth time and I can finally drag myself out of sleep and into the cold house is to bundle up in coats and boots, run outside and turn my car on so that in the half hour it takes me to get dressed, the car actually heats up and the windshield defrosts enough for me to see through it.

Before leaving to work, I spend another 10-15 minutes shoveling all the snow that the plows have thrown into my driveway out of said driveway, before I have to navigate slippery roads for the 15 minutes it takes me to get to work.

"I'll be broke before I'm warm!"

I am beginning to understand why my pay is decent in this part of the world (um... because no one in their sane mind would live here?!) and why everyone drives a 4-wheel drive truck (again, slippery roads). But little me is not made for this weather and this environment. I'm a poor sun-loving beach bunny, not a rich, snow-blower-owning 4x4-driving snow bunny!

I Want my Freedom!

Being a professional is not nearly as fun as I might have thought sometime in the past. Granted, with my new found cash I've been able to take a few more trips, go snowboarding more often and pick up windsurfing, but I have also discovered that there are all kinds of not fun responsibilities like going to work and actually doing something productive when I'm there, paying bills for car loans, electricity, heat, food, insurance and gas among many other strange and incomprehensible things like social security, 401k[1] , pension plans, etc...

Just thinking about all this is enough to give me a panic attack! And then to top it all off, 3 people in 2 days have asked me if I've started thinking about buying a house yet. A house?! Are they crazy?! I just bought my first pair of roller blades, can't we wait on the house?! I'm barely 26!

To be honest with you, I joke, but I've been thrown into scared hysteria. I'm young, I finished university not so long ago, there are countless countries and cultures out there to discover, waiting for me. I'll have time later to work on a 'proper' career if I want one, to be 'responsible' as people keep telling me to be!

I think I'll have my entire future to pay bills, and repay loans, and take out mortgages and worry about American citizenship if I want it, and getting that new barbeque grill like the neighbor has and giving my entire youth to a bank just so I can own things, right?!

Can't I just enjoy being irresponsible for now? Just for a bit? Can't I have dreams and a desire to follow them into the unknown for a while before I pretend to conform to

> " Can't I just enjoy being irresponsible for now? "

1 Retirement investment plan

mainstream society as 'a responsible and mature' (read as: a work-like-a-donkey-for-the-rest-of-your-life-to-repay-loans-and-pay-bills) adult?!

I'll have time later! I can't give up my dreams just yet! And if you think about it, must we really give up the things we want to do for the things we have to do?!? Hunh?! MUST WE?!

Virtual Escape

My window to the outside world,
my reprieve from this prison of wood and paper,
is a flat screen before me,
and through its bars I look out onto freedom.
My screaming voice
is composed of silent tapping keys,
orchestrated by furious independent fingers,
aching for escape.

Mortgage

I'm afraid of mortgage. In my mind, it's like a disease that you can never get rid of, but instead learn to live with.

The parents of a friend of mine just finished paying off their 30-year mortgage. They also both just retired. This means that it took them their entire adult life to own their house.

Now that they own the house, they're selling it. Just like that. They want to sell it and move to a warmer place that is more affordable, because now that their financial duties are fulfilled, they can actually look forward to enjoying life.

This is a concept that I can't seem to get my head around.

You bust your ass all your life so you can look forward to retirement when you can actually enjoy your life? And not even really enjoy because social security and pension are pitiful, you need more medical care, you have less mobility, and you probably don't really care anymore to go and see Pisa or Machu Pichu or the Great Barrier Reef....

I'm scared that this is what my future will hold if I stay

in America.

First, the endless job working hours in a cubicle with 13 days of vacation a year.

Then, the house and the mortgage, a ball and chain for life. Thinking of quitting your job?! Ha! Think agaaaiiiin sucker!

Then there's the car or cars, the family, the kids, the activities, the pool, the barbeque, etc.. ad nauseum until you wake up one day and you're 60 and all the things you've dreamt about doing in your life have to be squeezed into a few years in your old age...

Ma baddeh![1]

Should I stay or should I go?

It's a simple question when you're wondering whether to stay at the club dancing and drinking, or to go home and get some rest because you're working the next day.

It's not so simple when you have a work visa in the U.S., a good and interesting job, and no prospects of going anywhere else. But I'm suffocating, I have no love life, and I feel there's more out there for me than this. Is it real or is it *ghinj*[2]?

"I'm becoming the thing I've feared the most"

I observe the way of life here, I critique it, I wonder about it and I condemn it but, ultimately, I'm becoming someone else, I'm becoming the thing I've feared the most: a robot!

I go to work, I come back, I try to make more money, I save vacation time and take it when I can, I accumulate possessions and aspire for more, I look for love, I pay bills and insurance, I shovel snow and mow the lawn... I have, despite myself, integrated! My life has become a non-event and when I look in the mirror I hardly recognize me anymore.

But really, what am I looking for? Is it really that much more exciting to wonder what time the electricity is going to come back, to worry that the water I'm drinking is contaminated, to drive through the streets hoping there are no car-bombs today and to have to muscle my way through every line and road to get anywhere?!

---

1 I don't want! Figuratively, I say no!
2 Being spoilt

I would almost think so… I'm tempted to just sell everything I own, leave life, as I know it here, behind and go off somewhere on a completely irresponsible and immature impulse…

But should I?

8. Home on My Mind

ƒ ƒ ƒ

Airport Courtship

During one of my flights back to the U.S. from Beirut (via Paris), I found myself sitting next to a curious old man. He ignored my desire to read my book and struck up a conversation. He wanted to know where I was from. When I told him Lebanon, he perked up instantly.

Old man: 'I knew it the moment I saw you!'

Must be my thick dark eyebrows... I just smiled and tried to sneak my ear phones back into my ears as a slight hint that I was not a big conversationalist.

My subtle cues were lost on him. He started asking the questions Lebanese ask. Which family are you from? Which town are you from? How old are you? Who's your father, who's his father? Etc... I was being screened. I didn't even know why, the guy was old, and when I say old, I mean balding head, white left-over tufts of hair and a completely wrinkly face. He seemed pleasant enough and not too greasy, but still... Finally, when I had passed the test:

Old man: 'I have a 38 year-old son who's a neurologist living in Cleveland. Are you interested?'

What?! Excuse me?! You're wife shopping for your son on an airplane?! My Lebanese eyebrows shot up in surprise, but he quickly continued:

Old man: 'I really want my son to get married and I could pass along your phone number to him if you're interested. Look, he's this much taller than I am,' - the man was tiny, I was a full head and a half taller than he was, but he held up his forefinger and thumb like he had a Duracell battery in between them, like his son was a giant - 'and he's balding but

he's really nice! Really!'

I wasn't sure if he was convincing me or himself. I nodded my head that I heard him, but I just had to laugh out loud in, frankly, embarrassment! What the hell do you say to that?!

Me: 'Uh… thanks, but uh…he's too old for me…'. But what a downer it was for me! This was the best offer I had gotten so far in the romance department. How depressing.

Old man: 'Oh nooo,' he countered, 'that's the perfect age for a 26 year-old, really. You need a mature man.'

Unh hunh! He didn't do a great selling job. I just laughed again and kept quiet, running out of excuses way to soon. I can't lie under pressure. I should have said I was a lesbian, I was married, I was promised to a Sheik, something! But nothing was coming to mind…Blank. Just amazement at how blunt and straight forward (and pushy!) he was.

I finally plugged my earphones back into my head and tried to get some sleep. My empty love life was on my mind and I was so tired I couldn't handle any more crazy conversation. Maybe I would say yes if I was too weary to think up something polite to say… I couldn't risk that. I've been known to do stupid things when I'm beyond exhaustion and feeling miserable.

Weeds

> "Put us anywhere and we grow."

We Lebanese are like weeds. Put us anywhere and we grow. No matter the terrain, no matter the environment, put us anywhere and we'll survive, grow and prosper.

Name the country, name the city, you'll find us there doing odd jobs, having careers, raising families, enforcing the law, pumping gas, teaching languages, running governments, healing the sick, crushing *hummus*[1] and whipping up *kibbeh*[2].

I've heard of Lebanese-run clothing stores in Martinique and Lebanese restaurants in Puerto Rico, I've spoken to Lebanese Professors at Oxford and Lebanese Doctors in Baltimore, I've eaten at Lebanese café's in small American towns and

---

1 Chickpeas
2 Lebanese dish of crushed wheat blended with minced meat

large English cities, I've had my gas pumped by Lebanese in Washington DC and heard Arabic spoken by Lebanese on the streets of Montreal, I was sold *kibbeh mkabekbeh*[1] in Brazilian flea markets, and ordered electronics from Lebanese shops in Africa, I've seen Lebanese-run shoe-stores in Trinidad and Lebanese scientists in Italy.

There are towns called Lebanon in Kansas, Ohio, Indiana, Connecticut, Pennsylvania, New York, Oregon, Louisiana and Illinois. You'll find us in Australia and Russia, in Qatar and Saudi, in Ghana and Senegal and China and Sweden.

I used to think being half-Lebanese-half-something else was strange but I've discovered that most Lebanese are part something else, our culture is part something else, our ancestry is part something else, and we can make it anywhere.

People at work ask me what on earth a Lebanese girl is doing in the middle of Cape Cod, working with underwater robotics. I tell them it's in our DNA. We Lebanese will find the most unremarkable spot on earth to plant our feet, and there we will make sure that everyone notices us, what we do, what our culture is about, where we come from, and most likely where we're going next. Not only do we make it anywhere, but we do it in style!

We're weeds, we're survivors, and there's no amount of herbicides, uprooting, and replacement that can get rid of us.

Humiss

I think that if we all don't know how exactly to make *hummus*, we know what the basic ingredients are right? The Almighty chickpea, *tahini*, lemon juice, salt and olive oil, right?

Well here, in the land of the free, it seems that they've taken the freedom to completely screw our *hummus* up.

First of all they call it Israeli, second of all, they call it 'hunhmiss', with no accent on any letter, just 'humiss'.

Then when (not if) you see humiss in the supermarket (because humiss and Pita bread, which is regular Arabic bread, are now called 'health foods' in America) you never find a plain

First of all they call it Israeli

---

1 Kibbeh but bite-size

flavor, it's always Paprika and Red Pepper Humiss, or Black Olive and Feta Humiss, or Caper and Anchovy Humiss…

How have they managed to take a perfectly delicious, simple and healthy dish and turn it into a complete ice-cream parlor of flavors, horribly disfigured beyond all recognition of what it might have been at one point in the not so distant past?!

Memory Issues?

I was having a chat with my sister yesterday, complaining that lately I've been really missing home. So many routine things I miss doing. Eating tasty fruit and vegetables, spending a night out with friends in Beirut, having a nice lunch at a beach-side restaurant… The older I get the more I seem to miss home; it's weird.

Sis first laughed at me, then told me I was an idiot. She said: 'You don't really miss Lebanon that much, you just have a bad memory for the bad stuff and a good memory for the good stuff.'

Is that true? I mean, I do rant about things when I'm there, but I swear I remember a lot of the bad stuff… and the good stuff… I like it there. But I can't help wondering if she's right…

> **"So why am I missing it so much and dying to go back?!"**

I spent a month at home after finishing grad school. I must admit that the first 2 weeks I couldn't believe the inefficiency, the noise, the dirt, the dial-up, the pollution and the chaos and the ridiculousness of the political situation (As in: Have a problem? No problem! Just blow it up!) But honestly, after that, I fell right back into the pace of life there… it just takes some time to adjust, that's all. I think.

Right?! Or not right?

Friends in Lebanon are dying to get out. I guess I can understand that. So why am I missing it so much and dying to go back?! What kind of life exactly am I hoping for?

What happens to our immigrant brains when we're away? Do we really selectively forget all the bad things there? Is that why we miss Lebanon so much?! Is it only when we're not there that we want to go back?

Losing the Lebanese

I've been away from Lebanon for 8 years now. That's a long time. That's almost a third of my life. It's strange because the longer I stay away, the more I miss it, and the more I go back, the more I feel like a misfit.

Am I still Lebanese or not? If I don't go back, what will my kids be?

I went to visit my 3 year-old niece in New York (Did I ever mention I have a brother and his family living in New York?). She's talking a lot more than before, and her accent is 100% Long Island. She can't even roll her r's or say the difficult Arabic letters like '7' in *'7mar[1]'* or 'gh' in *'ghareeb[2]'*.

'But she's a quarter Lebanese!' I tell my brother in indignation.

That doesn't mean much. His wife doesn't speak Arabic, he doesn't speak Arabic with the kids, and the American attitude (as I was recently told) is: 'Well here in the U.S. we like our citizens to speak English good.'

What are the chances that this quarter Lebanese girl will have any interest in Lebanon? What are the chances that she'll ever want to visit?! Get to know the food, the culture, the language?

I want that. I want my kids to know Arabic, and be 'Lebanese' to some extent. I want them to feel they belong somewhere, even if they don't stay there! Will that ever happen if I marry a non-Lebanese guy?

There are immigrants out there that really make the effort; they give their kids private Arabic lessons, they send them home to the grandparents for summer, and they vacation with them in Lebanon whenever possible. It takes effort. It takes both parents being involved. It takes time and money, and a stable situation in Lebanon.

But what about the rest who don't make the effort? Are they losing the 'Lebanese' as well? Or is the 'Lebanese' we're worried about losing being transformed yet again into this new amalgam of cultures brought back by its citizens from around the world?

---

1 Donkey
2 Strange

The Point

At what point do we settle for what we have and give up the fight for what we want?

At what point do we exchange our hopes and dreams for the wet reality around us?

At what point do the wants and needs of society become our own?

At what point are our own wants and needs forgotten?

At what point does compromise become conformity?

At what point do dreams become impossible?

At what point does a larger paycheck end the quest for improvement?

At what point does adventure become troublesome?

At what point does travel become pointless?

At what point does education become redundant?

At what point is life too long already?

No seriously.

Is that the point when we can start calling ourselves mature?

A Change of Pace

I wake up early Saturday morning and am in a nervous rush to get to the airport. I don't want to miss my plane, and I am anxious to see what's on the other side of the flight. After all, I am finally leaving the USA for good and throwing myself into a month long adventure, looking for life in a place and culture I am unfamiliar with.

I already feel like a giant. All the passengers waiting to board are significantly smaller and darker than I am. Great. No chance of blending in at all! Guatemalans eye me knowingly. It seems like they are already thinking: another *gringa*[1] out to exploit our country. My paranoia starts to set in. As I groan and adjust my monolithic backpack yet again, a young Guatemalan lady carrying a crying baby in a sling on her back smiles at me sympathetically. I decide to forget all the warnings of danger

---

1 Colloquial Spanish for non-Spanish speaking white female

that I had read on the Internet and relax. It doesn't look like it's going to be so bad.

I arrive at La Aurora airport in Guatemala City and wait in line to change money, foot tapping and head bobbing with impatience. The elderly German couple ahead of me is having communication difficulties. I am too eager to start my adventure and get annoyed that I needed to take care of practical matters first. After finally changing money, I head outside to look for Raquel, my prearranged contact sent from the Spanish school to pick me up and safely deliver me to the bus station.

I step through the doors and my senses are assaulted by a multitude of sights, colors and odors. I feel like my heart has stopped for a few seconds. I forget to breathe while I take in the hundreds of people crowding behind a chest-high fence, eagerly leaning on each other's shoulders, trying to catch a glimpse of a loved one exiting the airport. Taxi drivers are indiscriminately proposing rides to anything with ears (sound familiar?!), street vendors offer up ripe mangoes and slices of pineapple to weary travelers and babies cry from beneath the folds of cloth as they cling precariously to their mothers' backs.

I am blocking the doorway, my giant-sized backpack reaching from frame to frame, and I come back to life when a heavy elderly man feebly pushes me aside grumbling something in Spanish. I hastily apologize and, remembering the need for oxygen, inhale a deep breath of stale fruit, baby throw-up and dust. I scan the little signs held up by people for my name but don't see it anywhere. I feel a twinge of panic rise within me but fight to be rational. Maybe Raquel is late, maybe she forgot, maybe the school didn't tell her, maybe they forgot. Oh my God, I don't speak the language! Breathe. Breathe. This isn't that different from home I tell myself, right?!

I try to appear calm and self-assured as I walk back inside to the tourist desk. I must not have looked calm because as I approach the friendly looking attendant, he asks if I'm OK with concern on his face. Was I not breathing again?! I smile awkwardly, feeling sick in the stomach and explain my problem. Oscár, as his name-tag says, offers to call the school for me. I scan the airport wondering what to do in the worst case scenario while he speaks in rapid Spanish into the phone. He smiles kindly as he hangs up and I know it's going to be OK. He says Raquel is on her way but running late. I am relieved. I hadn't thought to write down the address of the Spanish school hours away from Guatemala City.

"I have my first Spanish conversation by force"

I head back outside and scan the signs again, then the crowd. A harried looking thin-faced woman fights her way to the fence and tentatively holds up a sign, making eye contact with any obvious tourists around. Seeing my name scrawled across the cardboard, I wave at her with relief and quickly walk over to introduce myself. I realize in seconds that she doesn't speak English and have to make do with the little Spanish I had taught myself in preparation for the trip. I have my first Spanish conversation by force, throwing in French words frequently as replacements for my ignorance. She mostly understands what I'm trying to say. She drives me to the Galgos Bus Station and buys my ticket to Quetzaltenango (more commonly known as Xela, pronounced Chez-la) and wishes me luck. An hour later, I am ushered into the bus, and we are off on a 4-hour bus ride through a volcanic chain of mountains.

Heading out of Guatemala City we make frequent and crazy stops to drag people on so we can fill the bus. It is half empty. A bus attendant, hanging by one arm out of the open door of the bus, yells destinations to people as we race by, scrutinizing their facial expressions for any hint of interest or hesitation. At crowded corners, I watch through the window as he jumps down and pulls people towards the bus, seemingly offering them bargain prices. Occasionally, he grabs a lady's cloth-covered basket or a man's canvass bag of goods and stows it in the luggage compartment below as encouragement to get on the bus. It is comic to see people calmly tugging their belongings back out of the bus as the attendant tries to persuade them to get on.

During our stops, street vendors hop on trying to sell us chips, sodas, watches, pen and paper, or candied fruit and nuts. The bus driver then peels away from the corner leaving the attendant behind, yelling, running then jumping onto the bus while it is moving. He seems to enjoy the excitement and is always laughing once he gets back on.

We eventually leave Guatemala City with a full bus. People are crammed in 3 or 4 to a bench and more passengers are wedged into the aisles in such a way that no one can really move without causing a wave to ripple through the bus. It is hot, flies are everywhere, salsa music is blaring from the old radio and people are eating dripping ice-cream cones and salted mango slices from small plastic bags. Children tied to their mothers' backs are crying through mouthfuls of snot, and parcels are bumping around on the luggage rack above. I smile with the pure thrill of the experience. Life is happening around me!

We head for the mountains, still making the occasional stop here and there. There is plenty of farmland all around with corn being the most common crop. Farmers walk along the steep main road carrying bundles of cut wood and prodding donkeys; women carry children on their backs wrapped in large brightly embroidered blankets and balance baskets on their heads; children yell and herd goats along; dogs scavenge the roadside debris; and cows are grazing on tufts of dried grass invading asphalt. I feel like I just stepped into a Michael Douglas movie. Remember the Colombian village Joan Wilder and Jack Colton get to in *Romancing the Stone* after hacking their way through the jungle?

It seems like there is so much life everywhere. After the grind of living on the East Coast, after the obsessive organization, the hours of cubicle life, the obsession for possessions; after the countless rules, laws and regulations, after the mad rush to get nowhere, Guatemala seems like a heaven. People are doing simple everyday things. Things that are a necessity for survival. Food, water, fire, shelter, children… They smile. They laugh. They hug each other and say hello to strangers. They take the time to live.

The feeling of suffocation that had followed me throughout my last 2 years in the U.S. eases. This is what I had come to Guatemala for. To feel free. To feel alive!

I feel like I just stepped into a Michael Douglas movie.

ʃ ʃ ʃ

9_ Take Me to Beirut

ⴼ ⴼ ⴼ

At the Zoo

I'm really excited to be going back to Beirut. No like really going back, as in moving home to try to find work and be a grown up, you know?!

The American-Lebanese at New York airport seem fairly civilized, following rules, standing in lines and politely observing the no-smoking signs, actually refraining from doing so! Things are going OK.

At Charles de Gaulle airport in Paris, some French-Lebanese join the group and same thing; everyone is a civilized westerner simply waiting for a flight home. People stand in neat one-person lines at immigration and give you that precious radius of space around you that makes you feel more human and less cattle.

In the airplane to Beirut some strange and bizarre transformation takes place as suddenly all semblance of westernization evaporates and the primordial Lebanese is back. Is it the altitude? Is it the airplane food? Is it a change in time-zones?! Is it the bright lights of Beirut below that everyone is jostling to snatch a glance of through the windows? No one will ever know.

"Suddenly the Lebanese have come home." Suddenly the Lebanese have come home. Loud voices erupt all over the plane, a joker in the back says: *'Yi! Fi kahraba walla!'* loud enough for everyone to hear, then proceeds to continue to voice his every thought at the top of his voice, assuming that we all care very much what he thinks.

Wheels are barely touching asphalt when seatbelt buckles go flying from round bellies, and people are pushing and

---

1 By God, there's electricity!

shoving left and right to get their hand luggage first and barge their way to the front of the plane. The plane has just started taxiing so that when the captain presses the breaks you have armpits and crotches falling onto you from every side. The hostesses erupt in a desperate burst of 'SIT DOWN' and 'Monsieur!' and 'Pleaase *23ido!*'', begging the passengers for some sort of order.

The frenzy escalates when the doors of the plane open. If you're standing in the aisle, you're getting hand luggage rammed up your ass so you'll move forward that extra inch into someone else's ass, and if you're still in your seat, holding on to some shred of civilization and dignity, then you can pretty much forget about a gracious, 'please, it's your turn' from anyone behind you, and good luck!

When you do get out of the plane, it's a sprint to the shortest line at immigration, line being a term that is used very loosely, since it looks more like a herd of starved sheep finally let out to graze.

The effort over, packs of cigarettes are whipped out and lighters are heard clicking left and right, over the pleasant recorded voice coming from airport speakers informing us that we're welcome to Beirut and this is a non-smoking airport, in 3 languages to showcase our advanced culture.

After a good amount of calculated squeezing and pushing, I get through immigration and I'm off in search of my luggage. Me and my cart are standing literally 2 inches from the luggage belt when Bozo or Madame comes dragging her fat ass and squeezes it right in front of me, as if all she really needed to fit herself there was those 2 inches. Now try to see your luggage if you can, sucker!

Luggage has been claimed, and I am now disentangled from the array of luggage carts and clamoring pseudo-people. I get out of the arrivals hall and all the people who were once in such an extreme rush seem to have gotten to their destination: the arrivals hall of Beirut Airport. They're stopped right in front of me with their carts, kids and luggage, blocking any exit from the passengers-only area.

I dare to look out at the waiting crowd of relatives and it's

> Now try to see your luggage if you can, sucker!"

---

1 By God, there's electricity!

a veritable farm! People are standing 10 deep trying to look over each other for a loved one. And it's not just mom who came to pick up her daughter, husband, or son; it's mom, dad, sisters and brothers, aunts and uncles, the cousins, the maid, the driver and the in-laws too. They're here with *Baklawa*, balloons, bouquets of flowers, and, dressed to the hilt, like they're all ready for a fashion shoot, because after all, Rima has been living in *Bareeze*[1] and she will be so much more fashionable now!

I challenge you to try to make your way through these people when you get out. You're there with your cart, you haven't even exited the passengers-only area, but you've already been fighting your way through non-passengers for the last few minutes. The *darakeh*[2] at the corner is leaning on the wall smoking a cigarette and smirking, having given up trying to keep the order a long time ago; he doesn't get paid nearly enough to confront relatives of long-gone loved ones.

My soft calls of 'pardon', 'sorry!', 'please *bit mar2ouneh*[3]', fall very short of even making a dent in the chaos before me. After waiting several minutes for every member of the 12 person family to hug the returnée person and ask them how they're doing right there in my way, I suddenly feel compelled to call out the Lebanese inside of me. I take a deep lung-filling breath and bellow: PLEASE ZIHO!!! BADNA NIMROK! YA 3AMMI ZIIHHOOO!!!!![4]'.

This shakes some of them out of the way. The others are victims of my luggage trolley, as I viciously shove it into their clamoring bodies and scatter them like bowling pins. Suddenly, they turn to me and go '*Wallaw!*[5]' with a hurt and indignant expression on their face; how rude and inconsiderate of me!

I never realized Lebanon had a real live zoo, or circus if you'd rather, and I doubt it's going away anytime soon, so if you ever want to see it, head on down to the airport at Easter, Christmas, or Eid. The action is riveting!

> "This shakes some of them out of the way."

---

1 Paris
2 Security official (often police)
3 Could you please let me pass?
4 Please move! We want to pass! Dammit move!
5 Excuse You!

Unnecessary Education

So I get to Lebanon and I'm at immigration getting my passport stamped. The immigration officer is a very young, clean shaven *darakeh[1]* who seems to chat up all the women coming through.

He's going through my passport.

Darakeh: 'Where are you coming from?'

Me: 'Boston.'

Darakeh: '*Shou[2]*, you were studying there?'

Me: '*Eh[3]*, studying and working'.

Darakeh: '*Walla[4]*, what are you working as?'

Me: 'I'm an electrical engineer for underwater robots.'

Darakeh - looking really surprised and a little confused: 'You studied electrical engineering?!?!'

I, being pretty proud of that fact, smile and assure him: '*Eh!*'.

Darakeh, still looking confused: '*Bas lashoo? inteh helweh![5]*'

Ah! Now I see why he was so confused; I must be home to husband-shop, and if I'm decent looking it seems, there's no need to bother my pretty little brain with strenuous exertion, because who the hell needs an education if you can get a man without one, right?!

> Ah! Now I see why he was so confused **

You Want Taxi?

OK, I know these are a lot of airport stories, but to me, arrival in Lebanon is a fascinating phenomenon.

I'm aggravated; I've just been street-fighting my way through hordes of relatives to get out of the airport, I'm not sure if I've been complimented or insulted by the immigration officer, and I've just made it outside to look for my brother's car in the rain.

I've flown a total of 11.5 hours in a plane full of loud people, I've spent 6 hours in stuffy airports, and all I want is a shower

---

1 Policeman
2 What
3 Yes
4 Really or seriously
5 But what for? You're beautiful!

and a quiet nap.

The moment I step outside of the airport doors I'm assaulted by about 7 men. They're all yelling the same thing at me: '*Madaame*, you want taxi?! You want taxi?!'

First of all, who are you calling Madaame?

Second of all, I'm not frickin deaf!

> "I'm not frickin deaf!"

Third of all, is it because I look foreign that you're making a super human effort to speak English and to show me the way to a taxi because those 4 letters are really hard for me to decipher all by myself?!

I keep patient, '*La2[1], merci[2]*'.

I continue walking. Suddenly more drivers are coming at me: 'U want taxi?! U want taxi?' Maybe I'll want their taxi as opposed to the other one but I'm looking for the best deal. Ooohhh, sneaky me!

Again, '*La2, ma baddi* taxi![3]'

I've barely advanced 2 meters when the same thing happens. Now because of all the reasons listed above, I've forgotten that I should ignore them all and keep going; instead I need to release some frustration.

I suddenly stop and look them in the eye and at the top of my voice yell: '*Iza baddeh* taxi, *butlub* taxi! *Fhimto*?!?[4]' If I want your frickin taxi, I'm perfectly capable of asking for one so stop offering, OK?!

Amazingly, that approach is incredibly effective, if not a little overboard. The men inched away from my bellowing red face, sure that I had gone completely mad and decided it's probably better not to have a probably hormonal, aggravated obviously Lebanese Madame in their car for a long ride.

I'm home, I think to myself, with a little satisfied smile.

We'll See...

The greatest phrase ever put into use! When I was younger,

---

1 No
2 Thanks
3 No I don't want a taxi!
4 If I want a taxi, I'll ask for a taxi! Understood?!?

I totally hated it because every time I asked my mom to do something, to go somewhere, to buy something, the answer was always: '*Hallak min shouf[1]*.' I hated it because it was never a categorical no or yes; it left that little bit of hope dragging behind it so that even if you wanted to be disappointed or happy in anticipation of a 'no' or 'yes' you couldn't be because there was always that shadow of optimism, that hint of a possibly different answer. Somehow, just maybe, the answer might be a 'yes' this time.

And who is this 'we' anyway?! Who said there was a joint decision to be made? When did I get to voice my opinion about the outcome of the question?! Why must we be led to believe that 'we' are going to make a decision?!

Having recently moved back to Lebanon though, I realized that '*hallak min shouf*' was a phrase of frequent daily usage in everyone's vocabularies. A slyly evasive, non-committal little phrase that gave you the freedom of changing your mind as many times as you wanted or needed to without any consequences what-so-ever, because after all, the answer was never a clear '*eh[2]*' or '*la2[3]*'.

'You guys up for dinner?', I ask my friends. 'We'll see...' they reply.

'Let's go clubbing tonight!', I say. '*Hallak min shouf...*' they say.

I emphasize that this never means a clear 'no' or 'yes'. If I assume it's a no, inevitably I'll get a call saying: '*Shou? (So, well?)* I thought we were going clubbing tonight? Where we going?'

And if I do plan the wheres and whens of an event and have the audacity to make a reservation, then call to confirm with friends, they'll go: '*Ma la2*, I have my uncle's cousin's nephew's birthday to attend!'

At first I took offense to this phrase, I hated it and everything it represented. I thought the worst of my friends and went on a massive boycott of all further events organized by people using this phrase.

Ah, but now I have learned better, and I am so much wiser

66 At first I took offense to this phrase 99

---

1 We'll see
2 Yes
3 No

and happier! I have entered the world of Lebanese evasive pleasantries, and I now wield them deftly and with skill.

I've learned that it's always good to keep your options open until the very last nanosecond just in case an event more interesting than the one planned pops up unannounced. I've also learned to love this particular phrase with a passion, especially when faced with those pushy people who insist you pass by, on so and so date for a coffee/meal/shopping etc… and proceed to fend off every single excuse you can possibly conjure. In these situations, there is no weapon mightier that the *'Hallak min shouf'* missile. It strikes its target-bull's-eye and leaves your future open to you in a way that you could have only begged and cried for in your most blessed dreams.

So for those of you who still haven't figured out this little conveniently slippery fragment, it just might be the thing that is keeping your social life from complete and utter fulfillment.

Before We Die!

I've traveled the world, I've gotten a great education, I've worked on some of the most cutting edge technology there is out there, and yet, I have not fulfilled my one mission in life: marriage!

Every relative I visit has one and only one question in mind: when are we going to *nifra7 minnik?*[1]

Do they care that I have a Master's? Irrelevant!

Does it matter that I worked on some really cool engineering technology?! What the hell for?! How will that help me get a man?

Do they want to know all about the cultures I've discovered and the places I've visited? *Akeed la2!*[2] Why am I wasting my time around the world when I could be here looking for a man?

Are they interested at all in the group of international friends I've made? Well yes… Are any of them Lebanese men? Do they make a decent living? What's their religion?

Do they want to know all about the adventure sports I've

---

1 Be happy for you, i.e. when are you getting married already?!
2 Of course not!

discovered and enjoyed? '*Wlik* what are you wasting your time for?! You're 26!!!'

They say it with such intensity, with such alarm that I feel like my baby-making eggs are rotting on the spot and there's no hope left for me to get married, ever!

I try to tell them that I'm looking for a man, but I'm also enjoying my life in the process. They're having none of it.

'No pressure at all *habibti*, but *inshallah nifra7 minnik abl ma nmout!*[1]'

No pressure...

Ajnabiyeh

As far back as I can remember, and because of my looks and name, I've always been called an '*ajnabiyeh*[2]' in Lebanon. And because I never appreciated what that meant to the Lebanese, I always took it as an insult. After all, I was born and raised in Lebanon and I even have a Lebanese *Teta*[3] . How could they spit the word 'ajnabiyeh' at me like that?!

"Could I possibly be Polish?"

With this as a backdrop, and 8 years of recent American life in my pocket, I was starting to feel more and more like a foreigner and less Lebanese than ever before. I decided that perhaps a trip to Poland would finally shed some light on who I might really be, since I wasn't all that Lebanese and I definitely wasn't very American. Could I possibly be Polish?

I decided to visit my Aunt and cousin for a week in Warsaw. I had never been there and was excited to finally meet the people, discover the customs, the countryside and architecture, try the food and get a taste of what my father grew up in, and match what he had told me to the reality. Maybe somehow I belonged there and never knew it!

At the airport, I had a brief moment of elation during boarding when my long and complicated name rolled off the airline hostess' tongue like ice-cream. Then pure despair hit as she spewed incomprehensible Polish at me. 'I'm sorry, I don't

---

1 We hope to see you married before we die!
2 Foreigner
3 Grandma

speak any Polish at all! Arabic?!' I tried a big smile to help the joke go through. She just shook her head solemnly.

In Poland everything was different. It was so... European. The landscape was lush and green, the cities clean, neat and organized, the tramway ran at regular hours, and people were polite and courteous everywhere. The young would even get up and offer their seats to the elderly with generous smiles.

One night we went out to a special restaurant for some traditional Polish dancing. As we walked in, I was already looking around for something traditional, something that was obviously Polish, that was obviously different and special, but it seemed like a regular middle class restaurant. Simple tables and chairs, no obvious decoration, brightly lit beer signs, a small sparsely stocked bar in a corner and a band leaning against the wall.

We sat down and ordered beers. The music didn't seem all that different from typical western music, and in fact there were many songs that I recognized, but they were remixed to a different beat. The dancing, however, was a completely different world. People only danced in couples and, the man and the woman in each other's arms, they seemed to just jump forward and backward out of beat, twirling around occasionally and swaying left and right.

A few minutes into the next song, a guy from the table beside us jumped up and asked me to dance in Polish. I was shy and had no clue how to dance this funky dance but my Aunt said something to him and pushed me off my seat. I quickly succumbed after a vain and inarticulate attempt at refusal and Aunty's bony finger poking me in the back. I watched and followed the others, starting with delicate hops back and forth. It was simple really and I picked it up quick. Left forward, right forward, left backward, right backward. That was it. I had finally been introduced to the Polka. It was even easier once you relaxed because the guys got quite excited while dancing and would just fling and shake you around like a dusty cloth.

The next song had more oriental sounds to it and I was tempted to throw in some Arabic dance moves. They were so much more gracious than this hopping around! I got some surprised and disapproving looks so I headed back for the table.

Everyone had beer on their tables but the level of beer in their glasses was unchanging. Strangely, people were getting progressively more drunk. Turns out everyone had bottles of Vodka under their tables and either drank it straight or added it to their beer. Interesting, no?

Next day early in the morning, we caught a bus to head into a small village in the mountains. As I watched life go by through the window, I noticed several people at bus stops sipping from giant cans of beer while they waited for the morning bus. Where was the all important *ahweh*[1] at this hour of the morning?

The one thing that struck me most on that bus ride was the incredible beauty of the country. The grassy mountains, the sprawling forests, the perfect cities... But I felt nothing. I felt, this is Poland... nice...

But then I thought of Lebanon, I longed to be there, I longed to see the familiar landscape, smell the sweating sea and look up at the thirsty mountains. I longed to feel safe and comfortable and secure. I long(ed) for that feeling of 'home'.

I could see how Poland could instill that feeling in someone else, someone who had grown up there. How the rich greenery, the imposing trees and the rolling hills could grow in someone's heart and be home to them.

My relatives were great, they were kind and generous and loving. They took me everywhere and showed me all kinds of things but there was always a little something missing, a little something misunderstood.

> "I was definitely not Polish."

Suddenly I felt so much better. I felt so un-Polish. The *ajnabiyeh* stigma slowly dissolved. I suddenly felt so Lebanese that I started humming Sammy Clark happily under my breath.

It was settled; I was definitely not Polish.

Ghost

I slowly drift into consciousness to the remarkable sound of singing birds. Singing birds? I usually wake up to the sound of kids screaming on their way to school, ambulance sirens at full

---

1 Arabic coffee

speed, and angry car horns at the intersection below my house.

What time is it anyway?

5:30am. I groan. Curiously though, the silence outside is calling me. I gently push my cat off me and head for the windows. It's still dark and cloudy, the skies are only starting to clear from the night time depression. The city looks so peaceful. And straight in front of me, the one tree in my neighborhood, the one surviving mammoth housing a thousand songs, smiles back at me and beckons with a green arm...

I am somehow fully awake and for no rational reason decide to go for a run. It's 6am, what am I thinking? I'm not. And it's nice for a change. I gear up and head outside into the arms of stillness. We embrace like old friends who haven't seen each other in a long time. I love deserted cities in ways I can't explain. I stretch and get going.

Was it still alive? **

Usually I head away from the centre, away from all the noise and rush, up the hill to a distant quarter. Today I head into dead centre. I head for the heart. Is it still beating? Was it still alive?

I run past a few souls up early to battle their demons as well. I feel solidarity in their silent stares. We are on the same mission. I run past street sweepers, fatigue and worry weighing down their features so much that they can't smile if they try. A solitary cyclist speeds past, her wet hair flying behind her like a black nightmare in pursuit.

I look down often to avoid the night's accumulation of garbage, dog shit, puddles of urine and windblown debris on the sidewalk, the residue of the city's nightly prostitution of itself. An old lady rushes to catch the first bus of the day, her features knitted in concentration. Not a hint of pleasure in her heavy steps.

Slowly, the first motorists begin to appear; those people who need to be at their desks before everyone else. Resentful. Somber. Sleep still blinding their vision. My breathing gets louder, my footsteps get heavier. I continue.

Another pedestrian on his way to the bus stop huddles into his coat despite the warmth. A roller-blader in the middle of the street, looking upwards, for... angels? Rain? A private dialogue with God? I wonder but the thought slips away before

I can grasp it. I am thankful. I continue. An older man out for a run as well puffs past, lost in his world of endurance.

Finally, in the distance, I see what it was that had called me from across the city, what had called me to come pulsing through its veins like an antibody to a wound. The sea. The sea stretches out in front of me in hues of gray. I get to the sea wall and look down on the rocks. A homeless man in a homemade (does that word apply here?) sleeping bag sleeps on his backpack under the open sky. He looks comfortable and safe in his nest of nature. I almost envy him.

The waves crashing on the rocks play me a little tune and goose bumps make their way up my spine and linger at the base of my neck. The tune turns into a symphony as the seagulls join in and I sit for priceless minutes just listening with eyes closed. My worries mingle with the crashing sea spray and are blown elsewhere by the rising wind.

The first smile of the day decides to land on my lips. I slowly put my tongue out and taste it. Oh it is sweet! It tastes of innocence…

I turn around and open my eyes. The magic dissolves. The city is alive and I run back as fast as I can, telling my eyes not to look at what they see. Stooping shop owners are already setting their vegetables and merchandise outside. Bakeries are beginning to open, the smell of baking bread rising with the sun. I don't see anything. I just run and run. But I'm lighter, I barely breath at all. I can't even hear my steps on the pavement.

Beirut…

10_Under Pressure

ƐƐƐ

Why?

A European friend comes to visit me in Lebanon.

She's an outdoors person and she had heard so much from me about how beautiful Lebanon is, how good the food is, how nice the mountains are, how we have rivers and coastline, skiing and history and culture, so that at some point, she bought herself a ticket and came to check it out herself.

Her visit started out really well, since she came at the end of February, avoiding summer's high temperatures and overcrowded streets. We went cross-country skiing in Faqra and had dinner in Centre Ville at night; we visited the ruins of Baalbek and had lunch in Kefraya; we went to the old Souq of Tripoli; visited Harissa and stopped for dinner in Jbeil. We visited Sour and Saida and had lunch at the Saida port. She was having a great time (and we had avoided any major disappointment) until the day on which we had planned a hike in Nahr Ibrahim.

Nahr Ibrahim is a beautiful, beautiful place. The hike is a winding path between green mountains, fragrant flowers and lush trees. We walked and walked and, while she continued to marvel at the beauty of the little bits of nature in our beloved Lebanon, we reached the river side and walked along the path nearby, admiring the slight fog above the water and enjoying the gurgle of the river.

"We're in the middle of nowhere."

Suddenly she stops short in front of a tree. We're in the middle of nowhere. Nature abounds around us, flowers are blooming and the river is racing past. Beneath the tree: a mountain of black and yellow trash bags, some even closed, lying there like a nuclear growth.

'*Euhhh, Kat, c'est quoi ca?!*' What is that, she asks me, curious. Almost as if my answer would completely negate what she was clearly seeing.

Euhhhh is the operative word here because I had no idea. Where did this garbage come from and why was it here?! We were in the middle of nowhere!

'*C'est le Liban*', with a typical shoulder shrug, was the best I could come up with. This is Lebanon. And sadly, that seemed to explain things to her too. She'd seen mountains of garbage in the cities, but not out in the middle of nowhere!

We walk on a bit further, and we finally see the source of garbage: A rusty container masquerading as a snack shop for lazy picnickers. The grass was full of tire marks, where people's idea of a day out in nature was driving up to a rusty shack and having a sandwich of God-knows-what ingredients, and leaving the trash by the river side. I doubted *Sukleen*[1] made it there, and I expected probably Nahr Ibrahim would do a better job of the clean up than the shack owners.

" Why?! "

I'm mortified, embarrassed for my country and embarrassed that my people have done this. Why?! I have no explanation. Why?

Libanus Outdoorsicus

I've made the thrilling and exciting discovery of a species of Lebanese I call 'Libanus Outdoorsicus'.

I have nothing against the general population that is primarily into fashion, hair, make-up, cars, night-clubs, restaurants, drinking, and what everyone else is doing/wearing/thinking. In fact, I enjoy some of that on occasion too!

But I'm always pleasantly surprised by the few people who make an effort to get out into nature and get some fresh air, hike in the mountains, go for picnics in secluded areas, or, God forbid, do something a little more strenuous like rock climbing, cycling, or water sports.

I've met a group of born and bred Lebanese that actually

---

1 Lebanon's contracted waste collection brand name, or its workers who wear signature green jumpsuits

love being: OUTSIDE! That means they wear hiking shoes and go into the mountains to walk for hours, they camp, they climb, they clean up their garbage when they're done and they love and care about Lebanon's nature a lot! Is that possible?!

They go cross-country skiing and snowshoeing without littering the snow with trash and leftover snack papers. They go scuba-diving and snorkeling and don't tear out the plant life and harass the animal life beneath the sea. They don't drop empty cans of soda into the water or treat the sea like a giant garbage dump. They do paragliding, windsurfing and rock climbing and all kinds of other sports regularly. I'm so amazed to see this species of people in Lebanon, and yes, I am so proud too!

We have some of the most beautiful land in the world and we just strew it with trash; we break the mountains into ugly quarries for rocks, we dump untreated sewage and tons of garbage into the sea, and build ugly cement blocks on every piece of greenery available. It's so nice to see people who care about Lebanon, about the environment, about nature! Who realize that their kids will most likely be swimming in the same sea, walking along the same paths and will want to live in the same area years from now.

Go people! Discover, enjoy, spend time outdoors, take your kids camping in the *barriyeh*[1]; don't mind too much about what your make-up looks like today, or if you should get a nose job and whether your hair is the right shade for the season!!! Go discover Lebanon, and be nice to it! It deserves a bit of TLC, having taken the brunt of endless wars and multiple years of abuse under its many 'caretakers'.

A Camping Trip You Nut?!

Me: 'I want to go camping for a couple weeks in Spain! Want to come?'

My friend looks at me to see if I'm serious. She knows me by now though, and yes I'm serious.

Friend: 'When?'

---

1 Wilderness

"What is there to plan? We're going camping!"

Me: 'In a couple weeks or so.'

Friend: 'What?!? What do you mean in a couple weeks?! We won't have time to plan everything in 2 weeks!'

Me: 'What is there to plan? We're going camping!'

Friend: 'Well we need to book flights, hotels, trips, etc... that will take time.'

Me: 'Flights we can find online, and we're camping; there's nothing to book!'

Friend: 'You mean real camping? Like with a tent?'

Me: 'Yeah! I have a tent that will fit us, all you need to buy is a decent backpack and a sleeping bag. I have a Lonely Planet Guide Book - we're set!'

Friend: 'A guide book?! You want me to travel with you for two weeks with only a guide book?! You mean we're not booking things with a travel agent?'

Me: 'What for?! It'll be more fun this way! I've learned a bit of Spanish, we can practice!' I give her my best let's-let-go-and-have-fun smile. She seems to be thinking about it.

Friend: 'How much will this cost, I don't think I have the money.'

Me: 'Well neither do I, that's why we're camping! I've estimated our budget, for 2 weeks camping, eating, flying and visiting places it'll cost us about $1500 total. That's it!'

Friend: 'You've got to be kidding!'

Me: 'Well camping only costs about 5 euros per tent! Where's the problem?! It'll be an adventure!'

Friend: 'We're not pre-booking anything?! How will we know where to stay when we get there?'

Me: 'Well I have pinpointed a couple of potential campsites. We can call in advance if you prefer!'

She needs to think about this. She's nervous. The mere thought of going on vacation without planning every detail is too much for her. She seems very doubtful. But I have been living abroad for 8 years; she's considering trusting me, but veeery tentatively.

What's the big deal?!

So there you are! While most Lebanese behavior is characteristically chaotic, *halla2 minshouf*[1]-based and *allah*

---

1 We'll see

bidabber[1]-style, when you actually offer a vacation that fits this exact mold, you get a planner! The Lebanese are full of contradictions!

RUN! He Said

So aside from taking it easy, enjoying being home and eating, drinking and vacationing, I really am looking for work. Seriously looking.

I've sent out CV's to engineering companies, I've looked for research institutions, (ha!) and I'm starting to explore my university options, as in teaching and research in my field of ocean-related science and engineering.

I would like to say I got several rejection letters from all the CV's I sent out but no, I didn't even get that small courtesy. So I've started visiting universities where someone might be doing anything that could be remotely related to my field.

I went to a well known and respected university in Lebanon and scoped out a fisheries ecologist (not quite related but close enough!). I figured he could give me some pointers on what approach to take for applying for a teaching job, and trying to write grants for doing some oceanographic research here.

After introducing myself and telling him a little bit about my field, my education and my experience, I asked the all-important question:

'So given all this, what do you think would be a good direction to take for trying to open up this field here?'

He looked at me a little sadly, then leaned forward in his chair like he was about to impart some really important piece of information that only I should hear:

'What direction?! If you want my advice, go back to where you came from! Go back to the States, or to Europe! Run back! That's the direction I would take if I could. You'll never get anywhere in Lebanon as a scientist! You're wasting your education. Grants and funding?! Ha! You're already too American to be here. Run back!'

I considered for a second that he might be concerned that

go back to where you came from!"

---

1 God will guide us

I would be competition to him; I considered for a second that this was his way of remaining exclusive in his expertise there. But then I looked at his office, and remembered him showing me the pitifully equipped lab where they did experiments. Really basic experiments that required little more than a bucket and a rope... I looked at his tired eyes, his ragged face and the deep lines in his forehead.

I realized that he was probably trying as hard as he could to give me the best advice possible. He told me a few stories of when he was young and hopeful and optimistic, of how he came back from the U.S. with grand ideas of expanding research in Lebanon, and where he was now...

How depressing and how pessimistic. Is there no hope for change?

Viza *bi Tiza!*[1]

I went to apply for a visit visa to the U.S. It's time for a quick visit to my sister and brother, to see nieces, friends and in-laws.

"Quel honeur!"

I've lived there 8 years, I've been offered a green card, I've gotten my education there, I've proven that I really have no interest in becoming a citizen, and yet, still they pretend they are the most coveted country in the world and believe everyone would kill to get in and live there. Everyone is dying to become, wait for it... drum roll... an American! *Quel honeur!*

I pay the fees, I wait for my appointment, I drive to the embassy, I get hassled for parking, I get sent back to get new pictures because one of my ears was slightly covered in the old pictures and my face was not filling up enough of the photo; so off I go to make a whole bunch of new ugly pictures, and finally, sit down to wait my turn.

OK, fine! All this is no problem so far. Everyone has to go through this, so why not me.

After some hours of waiting, watching people leave, either ready to jump for joy or getting really angry at the interviewer behind the bullet proof glass, it's my turn.

---

1 Her ass! Figuratively 'she can stuff her visa!'

I walk over, confident I'll get my visa since I've been there so often.

But alas, there's a problem with my residency. I'm preparing to move to France to do my PhD, and so I don't have papers that prove I'm a resident of Lebanon. But my papers in France are not finished so I don't have proof that I'm there either. The woman interviewing me is a total b***h. She refuses to listen to a word, she snaps her words at me : 'This interview. Is over!' and turns her back and starts walking away. I'm furious! Not because they said no about the visa. Who cares! But because the 'ho' is living in our country, eating our food, breathing our air, and being rude to us! Who the hell does she think she is?!?!

"I hate America, I hate Americans"

My mind spontaneously combusts, leaving a little mushroom cloud above me! In that second, I hate America, I hate Americans, I hate what America stands for and everything they do or produce. I don't care if I never set foot in that country again. They can take it and stuff it!

I lean in to the glass window, and say really loudly: 'Hey! I'm talking to you! A little respect!'

She half turns towards me before showing me her back again. This of course gets me even angrier. So I do something that I can't honestly say I'm ashamed of: I yell at her so loud that everyone in the interview room hears me: 'Well f**k you, you fat cow!' and I stomp off in a rage. I am spewing hate! I hear her say something and all I can think of is a smug: well that got her attention!

People in the waiting room either look at me like I am totally insane or like they want to jump up to their feet and give me a round of applause. I'm not too proud of myself, but I have to admit, I am definitely, DEFINITELY satisfied. Consequences or not, I don't care.

Consequences Shmonsequences

I went running on Dbayeh Marina. It's a beautiful stretch of wide sidewalk near a 'relatively' quiet road. It overlooks the sea and you can smell the splashing waves. In the distance, the Beirut skyline shimmers in the evening sunset light. It's a stunning spot.

On the rocks below, little cats run around looking for scraps the fishermen may have left behind, teenagers hang out in groups drinking beer and whistling at passing girls, and kids chase each other from rock to rock.

As I finished my run and stood in place to stretch, I saw a chubby 10 year-old kid pick up one of the empty bottles lying near his feet and throw it at the rocks, watching it smash into a million pointy pieces. His dad behind him smiled like a proud father. Chubby picked another bottle up and wound his arm to throw again.

I yelled out at him with my curs-ed impulsiveness: "HEY!!!" He froze.

The father turned to look at me. What's the matter? the dumb expression on his face seemed to say. I ignored him and spoke to the kid.

Me: "What do you think you're doing? Why are you breaking the bottles?"

Chubby: 'They were here'.

Well that explains it!

Me: "You don't need to break them. What if tomorrow you're walking down there and you cut yourself on glass?"

Chubby: "I don't go down there."

And because he is not directly affected by his actions, f**k the rest of the world.

His dad grabs his arm and pulls him away, shaking his head like: let's get the hell away from this hormonal psycho!

It's an attitude that is very prevalent here and is seen in every action. Like driving for example. There's a bit of traffic? *La ijreh¹* , I'll make a triple line and squeeze into every available space so oncoming traffic can't move, turning cars can't turn and now there's a huge traffic jam. But do I care? No! Because *ba3d hmareh, ma yinbout hasheesh!²* Acting for the greater good seems like a waste of time here; let's just think short term, let's just think 'me'.

The whole idea that each of my actions has a consequence

let's get the hell away from this hormonal psycho!

---

1 I couldn't care less! Literally, my foot!
2 May no donkey graze after mine is fed

behind it, that it affects the people around me and eventually affects me, my family and my friends, is so ridiculous that explaining it makes you look like a nut case. I looked like a nut case…

The Lebanon Dilemma

I'm here in Beirut airport once again, boarding a plane to head off somewhere new, to start over fresh, leaving all that I love and care about behind. I'm tired of traveling, I'm tired of leaving behind my family, my cat, my friends and my belongings. My stuff was finally shipped to Lebanon from the U.S. only a couple of days ago. In the last 10 months I have spent 2 days in the same place with all my things!! I miss my books, I miss my sports equipment, I miss that cozy home feeling I get from having my things around me. From reaching for a book that I know I own and actually finding it!

After the initial shock of returning home and the first months of constant comparison between here and there, I've settled into a lifestyle that I love, in a place that I love. I've met so many nice people, made new friends, discovered aspects of Lebanon that I never knew, and all this I will miss so much! I've developed an even stronger attachment than before to my country, my people, my culture and my roots.

There's that feeling you get when you're home, in a place that is yours, that you can't reproduce ever again in another country. It's a feeling of security, of confident knowledge in your bones that no matter what goes wrong, over here, you know how to fix it, how to make it right again.

So why leave? So what's the problem?

It's the Lebanon dilemma. It's the all-human search for a better life. It's a desire to have a job that counts, that you enjoy and that means something to you, it's the quest to get paid what you are worth, to feel that you are valued for your knowledge and skill, to know that the years of university education and the endless effort in self-improvement leads to something more than just making it, something more than just mediocre. In short, it's the quest for self-improvement.

"So why leave? So what's the problem?"

After spending almost a year in Lebanon fruitlessly trying to find work in my field (or in anything remotely related!), out of the blue I get an offer to go to France, do some work and get a PhD in Ocean Science. Not only that, but I'll get paid for it as well. It seems that I am one of a few people with the expertise needed, and they actually value that.

I can honestly say that I'm torn about leaving home, leaving Lebanon, leaving culture, family and friends behind, but not so torn that I won't go. Human nature obviously overcomes human emotion, and it's human to seek more.

I want more. I want an income!

11_Vive La France!

ʃʃʃ

Call of the Sirens

I am finally set up in France with PhD in progress. I have my own car (a little 12 year-old Golf), studio apartment (I even have a balcony!), job and the all-important but often elusive income.

What's missing? Oh only Batroun and its windsurfers riding the salty waves, the 'wazawez[1]' whistling at girls on their little mobilettes, Pierre and Friends beach... the smell of sizzling onions and *lahm meshweh[2]* ... the bright bowls of *tabbouleh* and *hummus* sitting on a broken table between the rocks... But I guess you can't have everything...

I was sitting next to a depressed businessman on the plane here. In the conversation I found out he had missed Lebanon so much that he sold all his belongings and moved his family to Lebanon to start a business. He had since lost all his money and was now going back to France to find work. He couldn't understand why I was sad about leaving home. He told me Lebanon was like the Sirens in Ulysses... the call is so attractive and irresistible, you always want to get closer and closer. As soon as you're there, you get smashed on the rocks and broken to bits... He looked broken.

I was a little more optimistic. I had decided to write a proposal to the UN for a joint research project with the Lebanese Marine Sciences Research Center in Batroun. And I had just heard that my project was actually to be funded! Yay!

My French advisor was reluctant to go ahead with the project but I insisted. I explained to him that although our resources were limited (a bucket and a rope, and ... a microscope?!),

---

1 Teenage show-offs
2 Barbequed meat skewers

and we didn't really have a proper research boat yet (we could rent one from the cheapest fisherman or 'borrow' one from our Marines! I said optimistically), we could do it. At least there was a willingness to participate!

Why couldn't we do this kind of thing in Lebanon from Lebanon? Why did we always need to depend on Europeans to come home and do our science for us?! But hey, this was a step in the right direction and I was hopeful…

The first phase of my project is planned for next year. Can I survive a month in Lebanon trying to do 'research' in a fishing boat with internet once a week and practically no equipment?!

I hope I don't get smashed on the rocks!

Français Libanais

I always thought that in Lebanon we spoke English, Arabic and French. But it looks like the French I spoke in Lebanon is not français Français; it's more français Libanais.

That is to say that a lot of the words I've been using make no sense at all. Here are some recent examples of my floundering tongue:

Me : *Laeti, tu peut me passer ma jaquette?*

Laeti: *Euhhh…. Ta quoi?!*

Me : *'Ma jaquette !'* and I do the universal jacket sign of pulling a jacket over my shoulders.

Laeti: *'Ahhh ton blouson! D'ac! Tiens… '*

Blouson?! Haven't heard that one before.

We're headed to the hills to do some rock climbing. I want to know which road we're taking:

Me: *Tu prend l'autostrade ou la moyenne corniche?*

Julien : *L'auto-quoi?!*

Me, realizing I'm off somewhere : *'Euhhh l'auto… strade?'*

Julien: *'Tu veut dire l'autoroute?!'*

Me, that's *exactement* what *je veut dire!* *'Oui, oui, l'autoroute!'*

I've bought a coke in a restaurant and I want a straw for it. In Lebanon we ask for a *'shalimoni'* right? But I think I'm being smart and want to frenchify the word a bit:

Me: *'Excusez-moi, je peut avoir un chalumeau, s'il vous plait?*

Waiter : *'Un quoi?!'*

Me, starting to turn red and realizing I'm waaaay off again, damn it! *'Euhhh, un chalumeau?'* I pinched my fingers over my glass pretending to hold a straw and leaned in with my lips puckered in pretend-sippage. *'Pour boire avec?'* I was feeling stupider by the second.

Waiter: *'Vous voulez une paille madame. Une paille!!!'* He shook his head and went off to get it, probably thinking: stupid tourists!

My friend just sat there giggling at me. *'Tu sais c'est quoi un chalumeau Kat?! C'est un instrument musicale! Ou bien un outil de cuisine pour faire les crèmes brulées! Ma pauvre Kat!'* A musical instrument or a kitchen torch? Great! I am an idiot…

My friend's car is releasing a strange smell while we drive, she's asking me what do I think is wrong with it. It smells like clutch to me. She's a bit heavy on the gears and doesn't take her foot completely off the clutch when in first and going up a hill.

'C'est peut être le doubriage ?'

Lolo : *'Le … quoi?'*

Damn it! I'm doing it again!!!! *'La première pédale à gauche? Tu garde trop le pieds dessus!'*

Lolo : *'l'embrayage ma petite Kat!'* She is so entertained! *'C'est encore ton français Libanais ca?'*

I feel ridiculous but also amused. I roll my eyes to the back of my head and groan: *'Ouiiiii!'*

Lebanese Efficiency

I've been in Nice, France a total of 4 months now. I've had quite a few experiences and discovered a whole bunch of new things, but, I have to admit, nobody does the discovery and integration process like a 100% Lebanese somebody.

My best friend came over from Lebanon for a visit and if possible something longer term. The 'instinct for survival' gene in her is so strong that I can almost see it.

"The instinct for survival"

In her first 2 days here, she had already figured out the bus and the train system. I haven't taken a bus yet, I walk!

In the next few days here, she visited all the surrounding towns including Monaco, Cannes, Antibes and crossed into Italy and knows all the best spots in each place. I haven't been out of Nice yet!

By the middle of her second week, she had already made 2 friends in Monaco; one gave her a free paragliding lesson and the other invited her onto his boat. I know what you're thinking, but she's not *that* cute; she talks fast and she tells a good story. The only people I've managed to meet are people at work, and even then just barely!

Days after that, she's managed a job at one of Monaco's nicest restaurants, waitressing off the books because she's on a visit visa.

Within 2 weeks my Lebanese friend knows the area inside out, she has plans with friends, a job which she reaches by train or bus, and is showing me around, to boot! Now that's what I call fast work. Integration at its best and only a true Lebanese can show you how it's done!

A Perfect Day

I went to see a Lebanese movie yesterday. My advisor had left early (we're in the same office) and, since I was getting nothing done, I decided to see what was playing at the movies. Lo and behold, I was super-shocked to find a Lebanese film playing at a small theatre.

I snuck out of my office at 4:30, headed home, strapped on my rollerblades, and glided through the streets of Nice to the theatre. It felt great not only to be out and about, but to be out and about when I should be working. Ten times better!

There were all of 2 people in the theatre, and one of them walked out after the first 15 minutes. I didn't think it was bad enough to merit a walk-out! In fact, it wasn't bad at all, but maybe I'm biased because I was so pleased to relive scenes from home.

There wasn't much dialog, but a lot of emotion, a lot of thinking, and I think, for foreigners, a lot was missed. There wasn't enough explained to the outsider. I felt that only I could

Ten times better! **"**

understand what was going on (Well maybe the other guy did too). The streets, the nice cars, the crappy houses, the billboards, Monot, the cell phones, Raousheh...

I felt so much closer to home, but so much sadder too. My cheerful mood about not working was really dampened as I got to thinking how sucky things are at home sometimes, how my friends are often in the same situation, struggling for a little meaning in their existence... I know everyone struggles to find meaning in their existence, but somehow it is so much more pertinent in Lebanon because we've (they've) had to fight so much harder for that privilege, for that right...

The translation of the movie name wasn't quite right though... in Arabic it's *Nahar Aakhar,* that's Another Day, not A Perfect Day. It's a much more appropriate name, just another day in Beirut...

Viva la Viza

I'm not sure if you remember my visa fiasco in Lebanon a while back, but I find myself, with a slight pang of regret, having to apply for a visa to the U.S. once again.

My brother has just had a son and wants me to be the Godmother. I'm Lebanese, so attending family functions and participating is encoded into my DNA. I have to go!

My residency papers are finally in order, so I make an appointment at the American embassy in Paris, take a train, book a cheap hotel and brace myself for the worst. Whatever, I'll try.

"No problems with photos, ears, or paperwork."

On appointment day, I get there a little early and am pleasantly surprised by how much more respectful and polite people are over here. So far so good. There are only a few people waiting and my turn comes round quickly. No problems with photos, ears, or paperwork. Maybe it's the Polish passport. The interviewer is an extremely pleasant young American and is very polite. What a relief. The questions begin and after a few routine ones:

Interview man: 'Have you even been rejected a visa before?'

I'm a terrible liar and I'm incapable of hiding my feelings, so

I immediately answer: 'Yes, in Lebanon last year'.

Interview man: 'Why was that?'

Me: 'Well the lady interviewing me said I had issues with my residency papers.'

He looks down at his computer screen and goes: 'Hmmm, well it says here you weren't very nice to her.' He looks at me with interest, waiting to see my reaction.

In the back of my mind I think, wow, they even document getting cursed at! But then I am totally indignant as I recall the event and react to the memory with renewed fervor: 'Well she wasn't very nice to me!!! She turned her back on me while I was in mid-sentence! She was plain rude!'

He laughs at my reaction, at my indignance, and at the reason. I wait for him to reject my visa. Then he surprises the hell out of me by smiling and saying: 'She was probably menopausal. She's a bit crazy!'

I laughed at that. He smiled again and said: 'Come back this afternoon for your visa.'

> "He was so nice and I felt so vindicated"

I could have jumped through the glass and kissed him. He was so nice and I felt so vindicated.

That afternoon when I came for my passport I was walking on air. After picking it up at the door I flipped through it hurriedly to see the duration of the visa. 10 YEARS! Wow! This means that I don't have to do this crap for another 10 years!

I love you interview man! My grudge against the U.S. is forgotten in an instant!

Reputations

Tell any Frenchman (or woman of course) that you are Lebanese, and they will launch immediately into a rant on how much they love Lebanese food, how delicately flavored it is, how exquisite and fresh the ingredients are, how much they enjoy Lebanese culture and the tradition of the mezza, etc, ad nauseum. I get so pleased and I am so proud of Lebanon for that well travelled legacy.

Ask them if they've been to Lebanon and immediately you will cut down your enthusiastic audience by 80%. Lebanon is great from a distance, but in person??! Isn't it dangerous? Especially for tourists? What are the security issues like anyway? And well, there are so many other places to visit, we should eventually get around to it…

So up to now, this is all understandable. This is the exact reaction I got from an elderly French couple on a boat ride along the Cannes shore. I left the conversation about Lebanon there and we moved on to other topics.

After a few more glasses of dry white wine, their tongues loosened up and somehow we got back to the topic of Lebanon.

The elderly man leaned in and whispered a confession to me. He did know quite a few Lebanese, but he was convinced that most Lebanese were not only merchants, but liars and cheats.

His supposed Lebanese friend had embezzled money from him and left him in legal trouble. And that wasn't the only Lebanese that he knew of. Another supplier of his had lied and cheated to get a good deal, leaving him high and dry. In his view, the Lebanese couldn't be trusted, and if you did business with them, you'd be wise to count your fingers after every handshake.

Are we really like that out there? Please say no!

ʄʄʄ

12. World Cup and World War

ʄʄʄ

Hope

"I hate hope."

I hate hope.
It creeps up inside you
despite the fight you put up
despite the despair you'd rather hold on to
it takes hold of a part of you not under your control
and makes you believe in things you don't want to
then when things come crashing down in a big mess around you
it disappears until you clean up, then sneaks back in uninvited.
I hate hope. It's a fungus in the emotions of life...

I Haven't Spoken About the World Cup Yet!

Two nights ago I woke up to the sounds of blowing horns and screams of *'Viva Italiaaaa'*.

Last night I decided to be smart and didn't bother sleeping before the end of the semi-finals game.

At 9pm I glanced at my watch thinking, there it goes, the game has started. Exactly 32 minutes later, I knew that someone had scored since my entire apartment building slowly started to rumble and soon afterwards a tidal wave of screaming erupted from all around. My eardrums hurt, and I was sure men weren't supposed to have such high-pitched voices.

Silence resumed as the game continued. It wasn't over yet. I hopped on the internet (I have no TV!) and found that Zidane had scored. Great, I thought! Only the biggest player in

France, and since he's of North African origin, avidly supported by not only every Frenchman (and woman, please don't make me be politically correct!) but every North African in my neighborhood, not an easily ignored fan-base!

At 86 minutes, voices started to emerge again. I tried to glance uninterestedly at the score but I admit I was excited. Don't get me wrong, I love football. In fact, I play football with the guys at work. But I try to maintain some sort of dignity when it comes to these worldwide worshipping fests. And it's kinda cool that for the first time in the history of me, I am actually living in a country that could win.

Finally, 4 minutes later, all hell broke loose. Screaming kids were at the bottom of my building as the blowing car horns got nearer and nearer. It started out fairly mildly and I thought, oh, this isn't too bad, it's tolerable.

Really? The volume slowly escalated as more and more cars started circulating, air horns were blaring and by now my ear drums really ached. My head was pounding and my cat trembled under my bed. I stepped out onto my terrace because I just had to see all this. I wasn't in France every day was I? Well yes, but they didn't get this close to winning the World Cup every day did they? Only the finals to go!

I leaned on the railings and looked down to see at least 16 kids, all nicknamed Zidane, playing football in the small *place*[1] below. Neighbors (including little old ladies, cute!) were standing on their balconies holding pots and wooden spoons and banging them together like Chinese gongs.

Cars, typically VW Golfs and hatchback Renaults, zipped around the corners, horns blaring and flags flying through the windows, screaming *'Allez les bleuuus!!! Allez les bleuuus!!!'*. More screaming and more flag-waving from balconies. My cat snuck out and crouched near the railings fascinated by the scene.

Immigrants, riding bicycles and waving flags, screamed past yelling Zidane's name while teenagers on the street blew referee whistles in return. More cars squealed their tires at the corner, with the electric blue lights on the undercarriage hinting at the age of the drivers. Police sirens and ambulance sirens were heard in the distance and progressively got closer.

---

1 Square

An hour later a fire truck sat below my building blaring its siren every 3 minutes. This was not a warning, this was a celebration.

Two hours later, my head pounding, I could still hear the waves of car horns beating on the shores of my battered eardrums... thank God the pot-banging had stopped.

I hadn't seen World Cup fever since I lived in Lebanon where every balcony and every car is emblazoned with a flag of some country. It was such fun (sadistically so) to experience the storm that the World Cup induces in people. It made me feel closer to home.

As some of you may know, Nice is very VERY close to the Italian border and harbors many an Italian. Regardless of the outcome of the finals (France-Italy), I feared all hell would break lose here. Not to mention that relations between Italians and French are not that fantastic. What would this place be like on Sunday night?!

WC Aftermath...

I watched the World Cup final with a bunch of friends. Turns out we were 6 girls and 4 guys. Weird ratio! Especially since the girls there knew more details of the game and more statistics of past games and players than all the guys combined. Despite all this, I couldn't convince a single girl I know to come play football with our lab team.

Then there was the food associated with the game. I'm not crazy about the French way. Wine and rice salad!?! Whatever happened to beer and pizza?

"Go Zizou!"

Regardless, the French lost both the game and their supposed dignity with Zidane's momentous headbutt (Go Zizou!). The guys didn't care. The girls cried.

I got up and walked home.
Not a sound,
not a horn,
not a spoon against a pot,
not a cry,
not a whistle blow,

not a cork flying from chilled bottles of champagne,
not a pop from fireworks prepared beforehand.
Dejected fans walked home with their heads down,
leurs bouches en pont[1].
Others drove home angrily.

A few courageous Italian fans drove by blowing their horns, shouts of French-accented *Va fanculo!* halfheartedly escape from French pedestrians...

I felt sorry for the French fans because they seemed so sure of winning, because everyone said it was Zidane's last game and because the players were crying in the end (and no girl wants to see a man cry!); but was I sad?! Was I devastated?!

No.

That is a resounding, NO!

Why?! I would sleep tonight, and for that I say: *Viva Italia!*

Finding Hope

I haven't had the heart for anything lately with all the events going on at home, the new 'war'. The July war, it's being called at home.

Yesterday evening I went to a peace rally organized by the RPL (Rassemblement Pour le Liban) in Nice. I sent out an email advertising it to all the people in my lab and everyone I knew in France.

I was about to leave work when 2 friends showed up saying they were coming with me. Then another joined in. On my way there, another friend called and said she was coming. When I got there, 2 more joined us, then another with her 2 children and then another couple. All in all, 11 people came. Eleven people who knew little about Lebanon but a lot about solidarity and support. A Canadian, 6 French, a Luxembourgois, a Spanish girl, and 2 Italians. That's solidarity.

Then there are all the emails I've been receiving lately, from people I haven't heard from in years. A German girl I roomed with in Boston 6 years ago looked me up, worried, 3 El Salvadorian friends sent emails, a friend in the U.S. called

That's solidarity.[»»]

---

1 Sad-mouthed/ pouting

at 2am last night, a Frenchman I had met twice got my email from a friend to tell me how thoughts, hearts and prayers were with Lebanon... A friend from Scotland, another from the UK ... countless in France and the U.S....

The point is, I'm not in Lebanon suffering from all this but my family, my mom and brother and cousins and aunts and uncles are, and I'm worried sick. Not only that, but countless others, children, Muslims, women, Christians, Lebanese, Israelis, fathers, sisters... in summary: people. Humans - all united by suffering. Real live flesh and blood. These weren't abstract entities. They all fall under the same category, the same species.

I was losing heart over the situation, reading blogs where so many people were expressing hate hate hate for one side or another. Delivering accusations forward and back, and finger pointing and seeing who could go back further into history to find who started what when...

But receiving these innocent emails showing genuine concern for human life, brought tears to my eyes and hope to my heart. Hope that the world hasn't become a place where the cost of human life is worth less than nothing, where blood and sweat and tears are the currency for freedom; and where zeal and fanaticism (religious, territorial, patriotic, whatever brand) are just good excuses for killing, maiming and injuring innocent people, existing breathing beings...

I hope there are more people out there like the friends I have. I know I sound naïve, but I hope peace becomes the ultimate objective at some point. I hope thought and reflection make their way into the minds of the parties involved. I hope that evolution eventually makes its way into the Middle East, and we get to a point where issues can be resolved without splattering brains and bodies all over the place, without having our children watch their parents die, without having our parents bury their sons and daughters in pieces... Dead people can't understand, and the ones that remain maimed and scarred and alone can't begin to forgive...

I Hope All Your Loved Ones are OK

Dear Kat,
This horrible war in Lebanon must be so hard on you. I hope all your loved ones are OK...

I've gotten so many of these emails from friends around the world. I really appreciate and understand the sentiment that is being offered, human to human, but at some point they make me want to SCREAM.

Horrible war in Lebanon hard on me?! I'm in frickin France! I'm not even living it!!! I wish I were living it with my family and friends there so I wouldn't feel like a coward tucked safely away in my life and in my career.

Hope my loved ones are OK? Well, in the strictest social sense of loved ones, like mother, brother, cousins, yes, but what about my people? What about my land? What about my trees and the sea I love and the rich red dirt of the Bekaa? What about all the children in the South who I've never exchanged a word with, who I don't know and have never played with; what about their parents, scratching a living out of nothing to feed themselves and their families; what about my shredded country, my bridges, my *akidineh*[1], my fig trees, my olive groves?!!!

They are my loved ones too and they ARE NOT OK! And it's not hard on me, NO! It's not f***ing hard on me, it's hard on them. Shrapnel and broken buildings and steel and bleeding are hard on them.

So stop asking me! Stop grinding the guilt deeper into my soul. Send diapers to the refugee camps and refugee school buildings, or donate to the Red Cross, better still have a voice in your own country!

Don't send me transparent emails that mean nothing and leave me empty...

> Stop grinding the guilt deeper into my soul."

Peace Not Pieces

Peace Not Pieces
I've been furious for the past 9 days. At the entire world. At

---

1 Loquat, a fruit

humanity. At the lack of humanity. At the ignorance that is so apparent in the world of government, starting with the super-powers, ending with radicals, and hitting everyone in between.

Everyone wants a piece. Everyone thinks they know the best way to get it. Everyone who is anyone that is. Everyone who is a power hungry animal with enough drive to put themselves in positions of power and with enough conviction to collect daft simple-minded people as followers.

The civilians, the citizens, the people who don't care for politics, for wars or for power, the people who want peace, get to eat shit and die.

“I want PEACE.”

I don't want a piece, and I don't want my country and people in pieces, I want PEACE.

peace Peace PEACE

Is this an abstract concept created by and for ignorant oblivious people who want to have nothing to do with the dirtiness of the world? Who want to keep far away from politics and from religion? Who want to indulge in philosophy and understanding and construction of a better society and science and research and art and music... Is the only way to attain peace, putting ourselves in positions of power and having followers who we can influence? Will education ever open the minds of these people so they can understand that peace is a tangible achievable goal? Not an abstract concept created by the artsy middle class?

Be Careful What You Wish For

Ever since leaving Lebanon, I would read the news abroad, BBC and Yahoo and MSN, etc. on the internet, and wish that there was more about Lebanon there, more coverage, more info.

Now because of the war, all I see in the headlines is Lebanon. Everywhere. In every type of media: pictures, articles, videos and opinion columns, interviews with politicians and generals and lawyers and taxi drivers...

I now understand. News is not news, it's bad news. And the more of it there is, the worse the situation is...

I really hope I never see Lebanon in the news again...

13. Love Takes You Home

ƒ ƒ ƒ

Back

I just got back from a vacation in Lebanon. Did I care if there was a risk of a full blown war starting up at any time? Nope! There were priorities and I knew what mine were: I wanted my *man'ousheh!*[1]

But now I'm back in France. The same thing is going on in the world... The political situation in Lebanon is still unstable, there are still coup-d'états in other countries, world hunger still exists, poverty, global warming etc... and I'm still as self-centered as ever. Some things just don't change... After a blissful week in my beloved Lebanon, I am back to being a foreigner in a foreign land.

Back to speaking French, back to sorting myself out in this place, back to my real life. I got out of the airport and looked at all that is around me in distaste.

How can I look at the Cote d'Azur in distaste? It's where people kill to be, where Lamborghinis rumble along the streets with ease, where botoxed women invade the sidewalks with poodles in their arms and sexy hairless men in giant glasses strut around in white linen pants... (wait, this could be Lebanon after all!)

How can I not be happy to be here? To be back...?

Well, it's simple. There's something about being home, a certain addiction, an attraction, a pull that makes it the most beautiful place to be, despite the garbage, despite the political instability and the insanity of elections, despite the polluted seas and dusty skies...

There's something about sleeping in your own bed of years

"wait, this could be Lebanon after all"

---

1 Breakfast flat bread with zaatar and olive oil

ago, in seeing your mom in the kitchen, in smelling *zaatar*[1] in the streets; something to hearing the squeaky horn of the *kaak*[2] seller's motorcycle, to seeing familiar streets and faces, and hearing the familiar language and noises that just set your heart beating faster, get your breath coming quicker, get your smile to flash in a second and your stress to melt away into the heat...

Take me home.

Now I Get It

I've met a man. A real man.
I didn't meet him in a bar,
I didn't meet him online,
but he's definitely cute,
and he's definitely fine.

I've always made fun of Lebanese for coming back home to find themselves husbands and wives over summer. Spouse-shopping I called it. They'd go home for summer single, and come back engaged. It was fascinating!

But I finally get it! I now find myself in the same exact situation. I go home for Christmas and like magic, I meet a man I'm stuck on.

I swore once never to date a Lebanese. I'm not sure why. I think I was convinced we could never get along (me being an *ajnabiyeh* and all!). But somehow, my relationships with foreigners never worked out either. They just weren't Lebanese enough for me. Usually my culture (I can't live with a guy who doesn't eat garlic!) or their culture ('Why do you eat that weird soft cheesey yoghurt for breakfast all the time?!' NOT a Labneh lover!) would get in the way, and it was pretty obvious that 'future' was not a word we wanted to be using around each other.

But with this guy, we had an instant connection. He understands me perfectly, he's been to places I've been to, he's heard of things I've heard of and seen things I've seen. We

I can't live with a guy who doesn't eat garlic!

---

1 Lebanese thyme mix
2 Type of bread

speak Arabic together and laugh about things only-Lebanese. We share a common culture and a similar background. We both love village life and big family get-togethers, yet we both appreciate the stream-lined lifestyle of a no-nonsense country. But not only that, we share the same basic values and we understand each other like 2 peanuts from the same shell.

Could this be why so many Lebanese go back home and search for love there? Could it be that all those Lebanese (I'm sorry for laughing at you!) actually value their culture so much that they too want to be able to share it with someone? Could it be that sharing a common background and a common history, somehow sets you up for a better relationship with someone?

Long distance will not be easy so I guess I'm going to find out!

Cote D'Azure Men

I went outside at around 4pm today. I sat at the port to eat my apple and to get away from the overpowering cologne of my advisor, the hot office and his loud yapping over the phone, all of which I had been subjected to since morning.

I sat down under a tree at the water's edge and looked out into the distance as the breeze blew my hair and the sun sparkled off the water.

Then an ancient cadaver clonked past, leaning weakly on a single metal crutch with that horrible gray plastic at the elbow. I was just starting to feel emotions of sadness and pity when I was distracted by a large earring hanging off his rubbery lobe. I looked further up to a huge Einstein like bush of hair and suddenly had a vision of this guy 40 years earlier. He must've been coooool. Or maybe he was trying to catch up.

He passed out of view and in sight was another odd picture... a young guy, I would say mid-twenties, coming off a boat carrying one of those small yappa-type dogs, (the ones all the old ladies carry around and dress up) and he was nuzzling the furball in his arms, and whispering things to it and coddling it, all through his supersized sun glasses. It was definitely a picture of tortured reality to me...

I followed his trajectory down the walkway when I was

suddenly distracted by another old timer in nothing but miniature Speedos, straddling a bench on his boat as he lovingly sandpapered the mast (of the boat that is...). He seemed completely at ease in his minimal attire and the gut helped conceal some of the delicate areas. I felt like a pervert staring at him but it was just an odd sight. You had to be there.

I got up and strolled towards the beach nearby. I was looking for the more common sight of muscle-bound men in knee-length shorts throwing a football around, a sight I had gotten used to elsewhere.

A few minutes later I see a figure walking in front of me in a thong. The hair is short, there is no bra-strap or bikini strings across the figure's back, the legs are muscular, and the butt-cheeks are hairy. The guy stops and turns around, he's wearing giant sun-glasses across his face while tufts of pubic hair spill out of the sides of his thong. He's waiting for his friend.

I'm confused but I haven't come to any conclusions. I mean in Lebanon we have many a metro-sexual man, intent on being clean-cut, primped and manicured, but this is ridiculous. All I can say is that men in this country are definitely comfortable with their sexuality, whatever that may be.

Feb in Leb

On a flash visit home, these were my 4 days:

I arrive late Friday night and go straight home to catch up on family news and get some much needed rest.

Saturday I wake up, call friends I was planning to call, then head out to cut my hair (because all Lebanese women cut their hair only in Lebanon if they can help it!); I have my nails done, and shop for all the Lebanese yummies that I wanted to take back with me. Then I head to see my boyfriend (who is still Lebanese!) at his house, meet up with 'the gang', have dinner, lots of alcohol, laugh hysterically and have a generally great time.

Sunday, is a family day, spent peacefully and pleasantly.

> " all Lebanese women cut their hair only in Lebanon "

Who says we're ridiculous for doing sea and snow in one day?! **

We prepare a feast of *asbi nayeh¹*, *foul²*, *labneh,* eggs, etc. for brunch, have the traditional Sunday afternoon nap on the *marjooha³* , catch a movie then have dinner. Later a friend visits for the evening, we catch up on gossip and call it a night.

Monday I have a meeting in beautiful Batroun with my advisor in Lebanon. I drive out there early, get all my work out of the way, and enjoy a good 10 minutes just watching the waves crash on the jagged rocks. I leave Batroun at 11:30 with snowboarding in mind. Who says we're ridiculous for doing sea and snow in one day?!

I rush straight to Faraya, hitting the slopes by 1. My friends and boyfriend are working so I'm on my own. I meet a bored ski instructor who shows me around all the good off-piste spots where the powder is fantastic! I have a great time but get soaked very quickly since my gear is in France and I've improvised with a pair of jeans. When the slopes finally close and I am the last one there, I head for my car, do a little strip tease for passers-by while I change into something dry, crank up the heat and head home. It's been a fabulous day, and it's perfected by a hot dinner (*mloukhieh⁴*, my favorite!) and an evening chat with family and boyfriend.

Tuesday I wake up to go hiking with my brother and a couple of jobless friends. We decide to go somewhere near Kfour, we grab a *man'ousheh* on the way, and drive to Ghineh. We hike through the snow across mountains for a good 3.5 hours. The view down to the sea is breathtaking and the exercise and fresh air purifies the body and soul. I feel so good inside and out.

We head home to a huge pot of hot *kishk⁵*. In the afternoon, I call up the gang and invite them all over for wine and cheese. I argue with mom about going downtown to pick friends up; there's been a bombing and it's not safe she says. I pack super fast as the whole conversation is taking place, I'm annoyed with mom, luggage limitations, Lebanese politics and war.

---

1 Raw liver

2 Fava Beans

3 Swinging couch

4 Meat and chicken stew of a green spinach-like leaf named Jew's Mallow, widely popular in the Middle East

5 A fermented yoghurt—can be taken in a soup with meat

Boyfriend, friends and a buddy visiting from the U.S. make it over. It's a nice get together and we are all enjoying it. Other friends call and text to say goodbye. I feel loved and happy.

Later we decide to go for a drive and show the Americano some of home. I am in the mood to go north of Beirut to see Jbeil. We are 5 crammed into one car but we talk, we laugh and ignore the political situation completely. We wander around in Jbeil, at the port, in the old Souk and behave like 14-year-old kids. On the drive home we stop by at *Harissa*[1] and take in the night-time view.

It is getting late and I need to do some last minute packing before hitting the airport. We get home and I make everyone wait for me while I shower at lightning speed, get dressed and throw random things into my suitcase. Finally I'm ready and we leave. I hug my family, my boyfriend and my cat goodbye and wish I could take them with me. I feel a pang of sadness that my trips are always so brief and so filled with goodbyes. I'm tired of travel. I want a home and friends around me and my cat with me for longer.

We drop my friends off first in Beirut and then Jiyyeh further south, before heading off to the airport, a convenient few kilometers away. I've mixed up flight times and my flight is a little earlier than expected, plus I'm worried, as usual, that my suitcase will be overweight. Mom is nervous about the roads, the political situation and me leaving. She is preoccupied. I try to reassure her that things will be fine. Mom is mom and reassurance is ignored.

We get to the airport and I hop out. My brain is squishy and I am so tired. I am cranky on the plane, and throughout the flight back. Each time I leave, I hate it more and more. My consolation, I'm moving back home in May. Yay!

Non-Science

When I first came to France to do my PhD, I was idealistic and naïve. I was convinced that I could do science in Lebanon.

---

1 Lady of Lebanon, the Virgin Mary Statue- an important pilgrimage site or tourist attraction

I was convinced that all we needed was an opportunity and some money.

I worked really hard to submit a proposal to the UN for a research project all along the Lebanese coast, Batroun to Beirut. I made contacts with some serious scientists in Lebanon, we agreed on a collaboration, and amazingly, I got funded!

The French refused to hand the budget over to the Lebanese. 'We've had collaborations before', they said, 'and the money just disappeared. We didn't get any results either. We will control the budget!'

I was rather surprised, a little mortified, but mostly, just happy that I was going to do something scientific in Lebanon and feel like I was making a contribution. So I said: OK, control the budget. Lebanon said: OK, control the budget. The project was on!

We bought instruments, we arranged ships, we planned our research and by my second year, I was finally about to go to Lebanon and do research with the Lebanese. But that was too easy. The 2006 July war hit, scientists and researchers scattered, there was a ban on travel to Lebanon, and our research was postponed.

We rescheduled for the following year. Could we have picked a better time than May? You'd think we were psychic. Just as we were about to ship our equipment, the 'conflict[1]' near Tripoli hit, and once again, we were grounded.

We rescheduled for May of 2008. It had to be in May you see because we were looking for a spring plankton event in the sea with our little robots. This was our last chance. I'm supposed to graduate in December 2008.

By accident, our robot sunk over Christmas and my Lebanon project was again in jeopardy. I refused to admit failure. I borrowed an instrument from colleagues in the U.S., I planned every detail, the equipment was shipped, I was at the airport checked into my flight and convinced that this time I would succeed! Then my boyfriend called me.

'I don't think you can come to Lebanon.' He was trying not to scare me.

---

1 Internal strife between the Lebanese Army and Naher el Bared refugee camp Palestinian militants

'Why?! I've already checked-in to my flight!'

'Have you been watching the news?'

'No, what's happening?'

'The airport is closed, arriving passengers have to walk a few kilometers to get a taxi. Tires are being burnt. It's dangerous.'

Minutes later, the airline informed me my flight was cancelled for a 'war emergency' (at least I got a refund!). I turned around and went back to my apartment. Our instruments were stuck in transit in Dubai. My French colleagues were panicked. My Lebanese collaborators were bored of the routine wars.

We waited a couple days but were soon forced to cancel the trip.

My dreams were sunk, my hopes of doing science in Lebanon shot to bits, my last opportunity burnt like an old tire, and a missing crucial chapter about the Lebanese coast left a gaping hole in my PhD thesis.

Lebanon, why do you disappoint me so?! How can you let me down 3 times in a row?! What happened to *el telteh sebteh[1]*? I believed in you!

I've learned the hard way though: you can't make science make sense in Lebanon, all you get is nonsense; too many variables in a country that is the experiment!

66 I believed in you 99

---

1 Third time's a charm

14_ I'm an Alien
in Beirut

ʄʄʄ

Dumb Foreigner

Wo-oh, I'm an alien, I'm a legal alien…

I've finally moved back home. I stopped at a traffic light the other day (it was red) and I got honked at by 3 different people. One of them even had the nerve to lean out of his car and curse at me. What's going on?! It wasn't in the middle of the night, there were other cars starting to move in the cross-section, and I stopped where I could see the light turn green. What did I do wrong?! Then on the highway, I honk at a taxi driving on the white line that separates my lane from his lane (I was feeling crowded) and he gets furious, waving his arm through the open window at me (in a piss-off gesture), as if my request for a full lane was totally unreasonable.

Later, I'm out to dinner with a whole group of friends, we're about 10 people in total. As the night progresses, I realize that I am slowly suffocating to death. What's the problem? Every single person at my table is a smoker! Hmmm… when did smoking get so cool? Then, when they offer me a cigarette, and I decline, they look offended.

'Yi, ma bit dakhneh![1] Bravo, *3afekeh!*[2]' They say in disgust, like I'm some sort of vegan freak who only wears hemp clothes and recycled-rubber-tire sandals! *'Ya reit ana fiyeh wa2ef…*[3]' they say half-heartedly as they enjoy another puff.

When I stand in line at the post office and actually take

---

1 Hey, you don't smoke!
2 Good for you!
3 I wish I could stop…

a number, people look at me like I'm an idiot (*haram*[1], she must be *ajnabiyeh* this one), then they dance up to the counter heroically squeezing through people left and right, and reach over someone's shoulder with an envelope.

I think I've been living abroad for too long; I like the order and organization. I like when there's a system. I like when you don't have to fight your way through every situation just to get something done.

I like feeling like there's a system on the street and knowing for sure that if I wait for the light, I'll get through the intersection without 20 cars cutting me off. I like not having to muscle my way through incomprehensible traffic just to make a left turn. I like having my own lane on the highway.

I like the cigarette ban that applies to indoor places in the U.S. and Europe. I like having my dinner without someone puffing smoke into my face. I like coming home from a club and having my hair still smell of shampoo rather than of an ash-tray.

I like having personal space around me when I'm standing in line. I like knowing that after the next person, it's my turn for sure, not maybe.

I was a Lebanese living abroad, a foreigner who was different. Now I've come home and I'm Lebanese-ish, but again, not quite.

How do you live with being neither one nor the other?

The Evil Eye

The eye that wards off evil is a well known symbol in this part of the world. It is always depicted as this wide-open expressionless blue eye set into the palm of a hand or a silver pendant or a beaded holder and so on... They've got a version for every situation. I've always thought of it as a nice part of our culture but a bit silly nonetheless. Yesterday I changed my mind...

I was on my way home, driving on a narrow road that barely fit the 2-way traffic it was meant to sustain. I was on the right side near a huge solid bridge-wall. On the left, a black jeep was double parked taking up oncoming traffic lane-space. There was

---

1 Poor thing

too little space for a car to fit, or so it seemed.

As I approached the bottleneck, a huge old Buick came barreling down the road towards me. It didn't slow down until the last second, just when I was in the one-and-a-half-car space with my mom's car... Gulp! Did the other car stop? No, of course not! It slowed at the last second but kept pushing its way through, insisting on claiming the right-of-way ...

I had forgotten how aggressive drivers are here. People would have slowed a mile away in the U.S., and pulled to the side to let me pass in France.

So as you can imagine, we were 2 wide cars squeezed into a very small space (but large enough as it turned out!). I was concentrating hard on not scratching my mom's car on either side; I sat up straight, rigid in my seat, thinking it would help me see better. I frantically whipped my head left, then right, then again left, stealing glances at my mirrors and the sides of my car as frequently as possible, slowly inching forward.

As I got to eye-level with the other driver, an apparition from hell stared back at me disdainfully. An older lady in her 50's, hair teased to fossilization, eyes so made-up they looked like burning coals in her sand-colored, fake-baked face, her smudged lips thinned and her wide mouth sagged downwards at the edges and stretched wider in an utter look of disgust and revulsion. I could feel her damning me to hell, cursing me to eternal misery as if I were the one who had built the narrow road, bought her a huge car, built the bridge where it was and double parked the jeep just so I could torment her...

In that moment I would have given almost anything to have a bright blue eye swinging lazily off of my rear-view-mirror, the open palm waving a no-thank-you politely at the evil that this woman was hurling at me...

I'm buying one tomorrow. The Lebanese are wise: for some things, you need all the protection you can get...

The Rain in *Libnen*

The rain in *Libnen*
Is an interesting *phénomène*

We have 4 normal seasons
But for some unknown reasons
We just can't manage to remember
That in the month of December
It will surely start to rain
All over and over again

The rain in Libnen
Can really be a pain
When we hear rain in the news
We head out to buy new shoes
We water proof our cars
From the sparkplugs to the doors
And see how long it will take
For streets to turn to lakes

The rain in Libnen
Never goes down the drain
The water levels keep rising
And what is so surprising
Is that each year we are amazed
That the water comes down and stays
Instead of figuring out the plumbing
That will keep us all from drowning

Ski, Liban-Style

Everyone who's anyone goes skiing in Lebanon, whether they know how to ski or not. Whether they know how to snowboard or not. Who the hell cares?!

The equipment needed? Fashionable ski outfit, large sunglasses, for the ladies perfectly straightened hair and full make-up, for the men a good hair style that will showcase their 'bronzage' when they get back to school or work on Monday and of course for everyone, the compulsory cell phone and cigarette pack.

The experience? Priceless!

I stand in line for the ski lift, (and when I say 'line' I am o

"The experience? Priceless!"

course, just kidding, we look more like a bunch of bulls being herded into a barn) skis stepping and scraping on skis and all over my precious snowboard! A *Madame* shoves her son into my legs, then beyond and says *'yalla habibi, ta7ish shway!'*[1] Way to go *Madame*, I think to myself, teach your kid to be a *ja7sh*[2] from a very young age. They both step on me and shove in front of me. *Quel courtoisie!*

Once I finally get onto the excruciatingly slow ski-lift, a couple of guys on the chairs in front of me are having some chocolate bars and juice. When they're done they don't even crumple the wrapper before letting juice box and wrapper fly onto the virgin snow, like alien flowers. I can't help myself, I yell at them for dirtying up our slopes. I mean, we are the people skiing here, what is wrong with them anyway?! They look at me with a slightly manic expression and mumble through giggles: 'They fell from our hand...'.

I'm still looking down at the garbage, furious that some asshole thinks it's OK to dirty up my slopes, when I see a skier suddenly stop mid-slope, frantically open up his jacket like there's a bee stuck in there, and whip out his cell phone before yelling loudly: *'Allo?!, Eh! Ana bi Faraya!'*.

At the top of the slope, I'm getting my snowboard strapped on when a guy in skis beside me *3ala rawa2*[3] slides out a much needed cigarette and lights up. He inhales deeply on the smoke, as if he's inhaling the fresh air of the mountains, and looks around like he's appreciating the beauty of the place before he puffs out a mushroom cloud of white poison.

Finally, here I am flying downhill on my snowboard, loving the speed and the quality of the snow, focusing and making my turns on the steep terrain, when I see a girl decked out in new clothes, sun glasses and skis, tumbling head first down the slope, screaming, and breaking her fall with her face. Her coiffed hair is all over the place. Her ski falls off, and her sunglasses are crushed to her chest.

I rush down to help but she waves me away angrily. She

---

1 Come on honey, shove a little!
2 Animal
3 Calmly

zips out her cell phone and immediately starts to *sharmet[1]* Tony for bringing her here in the first place.

I decide that since everyone is having such a great time on the slopes, I will probably head out *hors-piste* next time and enjoy the peace off the slopes.

Commanding Authority

My sister and I went into 'downtown' this evening and strolled through the newly re-opened restaurants and cafés lining the pedestrian walkways. We were craving a Cocktail *Shi2af[2]* and the cafés downtown usually have a nice atmosphere.

Very soon we chose a place we liked and as we headed for a perfect table, we were cut off by an eager looking waiter offering us a different table with no view of the Spain-Russia football game. 'But we want to watch the game!' we told him.

He blubbered at us, stumbling from one excuse to another. We understood that they didn't want us sitting there, but we insisted and finally, in exasperation, they let us stay, but not before making it clear that we had to leave by 8:30 because the table was reserved. OK fine! Why is it that when a guy walks in they are immediately more cordial? As in: *Tfaddal Monsieur?[3]*

But no cocktail *shi2af* on the menu, so we headed for another café close by.

The hostess asked me: 'Table for two?'

After the previous experience, I said: 'Yes please. Where would you like us to sit?'

Hostess: 'Oh anywhere you like! Pick anywhere!'

So we pick a corner table and before our jeans even touch the seat, 4 waiters swoop down upon us, babbling something about us not being able to sit there and maybe this table was better, blah blah, blah. Fine! We're getting exasperated but we move again.

Moving tables is not a problem for me you see but I just don't understand how to command authority here. I mean

---

1 Curse
2 A fruit cocktail with chunks of fruit, clotted cream, honey and nuts
3 Can I help you sir?

there's a clear difference between people kissing ass and people respecting you... or at least respecting your authority. Sis says that because I'm a woman (30 mind you!) I need to dress like a 'madame', (no jeans and crossed legs on seat apparently) throw money around like I'm filthy rich, and look like I'm nauseated from the mere sight of them... This is the common attitude to adopt here, completing any outfit of heels and full make-up.

So is it only money and males that command authority in this country?!

I tried looking snotty as Sis snapped a picture of me but instead a waiter came over and asked: 'I make it one for you?'[1]

Ladies Night

I was out clubbing last night with a few girlfriends. It was ladies night, the champagne was flowing AND a decent band was even playing live. Who could resist?!

Naturally women flock to this popular venue in hordes to get drunk, meet a man, and/or show off their latest boob job. And naturally the guys follow to check out the latest boobs on the market and see what they can go home with. So while standing out of reach on a corner table, I noticed that the shopping men could be classified in categories. Here are the main ones:

The macho man

First of all, make sure you fall in the category of the macho man. This means you've recently been in the gym every day, you've got giant biceps, you're wearing a very small T-shirt and A LOT of designer cologne, and your pecs are so ripped that they can reach out and shake your hand. Make sure your hair is properly gelled back and if you can manage, wear cool sunglasses. Walk up to a cute girl like you own her, grab her and dance with her. You're set.

The side-dish

These are the guys who let the girl come to them. They stand at the bar with a drink, facing the dance floor, and star

---

1 Literal translation for 'shall I take it for you' from Arabic (Bekhidlik yeha?)

at a number of selected girls until one of them gets some courage. She'll dance up to whoever she thinks looks best, smile coyly, look down at her chest, then look up and give a 'you-want-some?' smile. Then she'll flutter her eyelids and turn around shyly. You can either risk waiting till she tries again or you can get out there and dance with her. There's a chance that you've hit the jackpot. But don't be sure. Remember, women like to try things on for size first…

The desperate talkers

Also called the window shoppers because they do a lot of looking but don't get much of the merchandise. They stand in a strategic spot next to the women's bathroom and as women inevitably line up for a pee they ask a number of cryptic questions until they get lucky:

- What's your name? (Translation: If you tell me it means you like me!)

- Where are you from? (Translation: Please say Romania or Russia, please!)

- Are you here on holiday? (Translation: Are you looking for some casual sex or do you actually live here and have a reputation to maintain?)

The smooth dancers

These guys slowly walk up to an unsuspecting girl and start dancing with her behind her back. (Heh heh heh. Very sly. I'm dancing with her but she doesn't know it yet!) Then they get excited about this thought and start dancing closer, bumping their groin into her occasionally and grabbing her by the unspecified area between her knees and armpits that is known as the waist in a man's dictionary, and shake her around like a salt shaker, helping her dance and showing off their mastery of rhythm. Finally, for the coup fatal, they snuggle up their whole body to her and start writhing like a suffering worm under a hot light bulb.

One of two things will happen:

a) If the girl is desperate/drunk/blind/or actually likes them, she'll flutter her butterfly lashes at them and get jiggy with it.

b) If the girl is not drunk enough yet/has decent eye-sight/a sense of rhythm/or likes to know their name before they feel her up, then she'll very likely push them away/turn her back on them/or scowl very nastily (and may throw in a pretty word or two).

The dancing queen

This is the guy who comes to ladies' night because he knows that the men will come. He's here to check out the men, and to enjoy some free-spirited dancing with the ladies. Need I say more?

A double Standard Please!

A Lebanese friend of mine living in Canada came to visit us in Lebanon. He brought his wife and his son with him. He's married to a wonderful girl from the Philippines, a top consultant for a management firm in Vancouver. Their son is the most adorable creature ever.

They decided to stay at a beach resort to enjoy the full benefits of Lebanon in summer: the beach, the pools, the service, the food, the restrictions on Filipinas...

-wait a second! What?!

Alyssa was taking her son into the pool. Her feet were barely covered to the ankles in water when a lifeguard came running up to her spewing anger. 'Hey, you're not allowed in the water!'

'What? I'm taking my son into the water.' Her English was far superior to his, but he assumed she meant 'boy she was taking care of' and not her real son.

'His mother and father can take him, you're not allowed in the water.'

'I am his mother!'

Our friend comes running up at this point: *'Shou fi?*[1]' and he puts his arm around his wife.

'Mamnou3 el binit tfout 3al may[2].' is all the lifeguard knew how to say. Any objections were waved off with: 'that's the rule set by the administration. Talk to them if you have a problem.'

It seems this rule was demanded by the residents of the chalets at the resort. They insisted it be strictly enforced.

"I am his mother!"

---

1 What's going on?
2 The girl (implied, domestic worker) is not allowed in the water!

But I don't get it. All I saw around me were Filipina women holding babies, feeding babies, walking babies, breathing on babies, taking care of babies day in day out while the mothers manicured their nails, drank coffee with neighbors and denied the fact that they were mothers at all. The Filipinas ran after the toddlers that rolled around in the dirt, disciplined them for bad behavior and cleaned the poop they occasionally left in the kiddy pool while their mothers totally ignored their offspring.

Then suddenly the mothers were WORRIED that these women were not clean enough to swim in the same water that they swim in?! Because these women work for them and are somehow inferior in status?

Of course! We are the nation of ridiculous double standards. In fact, double standards are standard here!

15. There's No Place like Home

ʃʃʃ

Neighbourhood Watch

In the U.S. they have a neighbourhood watch, where the whole community reports on suspicious behaviour to keep the neighbourhood safe. In Lebanon, we have the 'neighbourhood watch' too, but here they're watching you! This watchful community spirit is not formalized as an institution with meetings and action plans, but it runs just as effectively if not more so than any official body. People are always observing movements in their neighbourhoods either on the sly or from more conspicuous outposts (street-facing chairs positioned strategically outside stores, cafes, homes for example.)

Living abroad for so long I've learned to love my independence, my privacy and my freedom.

Over there you have your own car and your own schedule, you do your own thing and organize your house the way you like it. Nobody asks: Where are you going? With who? What time will you be back? Have you eaten? Nobody says: Take a jacket, it's cold outside. Don't be late, you have work tomorrow. *Dahra heyk?! Shou ra7 i oulo 3annik el jiran?*[1]

Life is peachy (almost). But you're away from home, family and friends, and you miss them.

So you get back to Lebanon, to your parental home and you're sharing a car with your brother (who hates sharing a car). Your every move is monitored by your parents, your extended family, your neighbours, their extended family, and

---

1 You're going out like that?! What will the neighbors say?

the shop owner below your house.

The *jiran*[1] see, hear and know everything there is to know about you. If you leave, you're observed, if you come home late, it's a scandal, if you're seen with a guy friend your reputation is dragged through the dirt, if you wear something a bit more revealing than normal, the color of your bra makes it to Facebook; nothing you do goes unnoticed!

One year when I came home for a visit, I was at the shop around the corner buying *Labneh*. At the counter, the checkout girl smiles and goes: *'Hi! Keefik?*[2] You're back?! How's America?! How are your studies going?'

I can swear to you right now that I had never met or even seen this girl before. 'Uh, are you sure you know me?'

'Eh akeed![3] Isn't your sister there too? The one with the curly hair? How is she doing? Is she back as well?'

Holy yikes! She knows my whole family story and I've never even met her?! I was very seriously spooked.

Every time you see that curtain in the house from across move, know there's someone behind it watching you. Every time you see someone standing on their balcony harmlessly smoking a cigarette, they're tracking your movements. Every lady innocently hanging her laundry outside is secretly keeping record of what time you leave and come back to your house, and every shop keeper idly swatting flies as he waits for customers is monitoring who you're spending time with most.

You want information on someone in your neighbourhood? Move over surveillance cameras, miniature microphones, and spy outfits, just ask the neighbours! They'll give times, dates, people seen with, colours of outfits and even the shade of eye-shadow worn!

Family

Through a strange and not-so-unusual series of exoduses and home-comings over the past generations, my family now

---

1 Neighbors
2 How are you?
3 Yes for sure!

includes Lebanese-Jamaican, Lebanese-Polish, Lebanese-Australian, Lebanese-Italian, Lebanese-American, Lebanese-English, Irish, Welsh and German members. Talk about confusing!

Somehow though, when we reunite only the Lebanese in us expresses itself at our gatherings. Every single event revolves around preparing, cooking, eating, getting ready for, or going out to food-related events.

As usual in such reunions, advice starts flying around the moment two people open their mouths: (*wlek lah ya ibneh[1]*, how many times do I have to tell you *jarrit el ghaz[2]* is installed like this!); strong opinions of should and shouldn't are frequently voiced (*Wlik us7a![3]* You don't fry an egg from the village in regular oil!); there is always the 'expert' of the subject ready to bless us with his knowledge (*Ma s2alouneh[4]*, the problem of the Middle East is easy! Let me tell you!); there are the occasional low blows to someone's ego (You're so flat chested, *leysh terka 7alik heyk?![5]*); and the embarrassing childhood photographs that get circulated where they can be best used as blackmail material; old stories of past glories are visited and revisited a thousand times (*Ammo* George yelling from the kitchen: Tony, *btitzakar[6]* when you were 14 and you stole your uncle's car *ou ta7bashta?![7]*); and throughout all this, there is the hoard of children aged 6 and under running around screaming, crying or demanding attention in one way or another (*Mama, baddna bouza![8]*).

Action plans and timetables are devised and revised but never implemented, conflicts in project-planning and eating scheduling cause as much discord as a civil war, before everyone ends up doing their own thing in a huff.

No one ever knows how long is too short for this reunion

<blockquote>"the problem of the Middle East is easy!"</blockquote>

---

1 No my boy!
2 The gas cylinder
3 Don't you dare!
4 Well ask me!/ similar to 'if you ask me' but with more imploring to be asked 'just ask me'!
5 Why have you left yourself like this?
6 Remember
7 You crashed it
8 We want ice-cream

but they're sure that more than a week is too much. Everyone usually looks forward to the event with a perverse and almost sadistic knowledge that there will be many painful moments amid the few fun ones.

In the closing stage, there is much hugging and handshaking and kissing and crying, tentative plans are made for the next meeting, promises of more frequent visits are handed out like *baklawa* and finally people gladly, but a little sadly, return to their everyday lives.

Ana Abl!

At least one in two Lebanese generally suffer from the *Ana abl[1]* syndrome.

In every public place or situation that involves crowds, this syndrome kicks in and you can see it in people's eyes, as the mantra plays over in their minds: *Ana abl, ana abl, ana abl!* Someone is always more important and more special than you are, and therefore they should be: *abl!*

Try to stand in a line (like they do in every country west of Greece!) for anything from buying bread to paying your phone bill. People will cut in left and right, with random phrases, 'sorry *bas takkeh[2]*, they're waiting for me in the car', '*bas sou2al zgheer[3]*', or just 'Sorry!' with no explanation attached, or they just barge through and sneak in front of you pretending not to see you at all, as if you just won't notice the 2 meters tall person pushing past.

And if you say, 'Excuse me, but there's a line here, please wait in it like everyone else.', they'll look back at the line of 15 people in shock! Hey, where did all those people come from?! Then they'll go, '*Ahh[4]*' and give you a dirty look before trying to squeeze in front of someone else who's less vocal or won't notice.

Again driving, same thing. Everyone on the road has the

Excuse me, but there's a line here »

---

1 Me first
2 Just one second
3 Just a small question
4 Typical Lebanese exclamation meaning 'Oh!'

'*Ana Abl*' syndrome.

There'll be gridlock traffic as far as the eye can see, no one is going anywhere, and some dick will drive his BMW onto the sidewalk and off again, just to get one car ahead, just to cut in front of you or the next guy. Bravo! You got 2 meters ahead of me but scraped the hell out of your pretty rims in the process. Why?! Because, ANA ABL!

The *ana-abls* will create 3 extra lanes per road, they will cut-off oncoming traffic and block entire intersections, they will cause more traffic than there originally was all in their effort to be first in line.

All that to get where? Nowhere! Because another selfish jackass is going to come and do the exact same thing to you, my *ana-abl* friend.

Time

" It shrinks and expands without warning or alarm. "

Time in Lebanon is a phenomenon to marvel at. It shrinks and expands without warning or 'alarm'.

When the cashier at the bank tells you: *yalla d2i2a*[1], you can be sure that what they mean is, 'we might finish within the hour'. If you ask your hairdresser how long the wait is, he'll say: 'only 15 minutes, sit, sit!' If you ask again how long after having waited for an hour and a half, he'll say: '*ma iltillik*[2], 15 minutes!' and get huffy with you for not getting it.

When my boyfriend says: 'OK, we'll go in 5 minutes', he doesn't really mean 5 minutes according to a proper clock, he means we'll go sometime in the near future, and most likely today. But then when he's trying to remember the last time we went out for dinner together, '*just mbere7*[3]' is his version of 'so long ago I can't remember'.

When an employee tells their boss: 'I've been working on this ALL morning', he really means: 'I worked on it before lunch'. BUT, when it's time to fill out the time sheet, a half-hour job grows into a 6-hour marathon and hello overtime!

---

1 Just one minute
2 I already told you
3 Yesterday

If you've scheduled a meeting at 10am and your appointment shows up around 11:45am, do they apologize for being late? Of course not. You said around 10, right?

Sometimes you can sit in traffic for 2 hours because the cars in front of you are in no rush to get anywhere, the taxi driver has stopped in the middle of the highway to pick someone up, and the guy in the BMW in front of you is driving slowly so he can check out the girls in the Rav4. But then again, if you take longer than a nanosecond to get going at a green traffic light, everyone behind you will start honking for you to get the hell on with it and the black Range Rover will almost run you over to get to the gas station 100 meters ahead.

You may not appreciate the Lebanese sense of time in all these situations. But when you're out to lunch on a lazy Sunday afternoon and your reservation is for 1pm but you get there at 3, you take up a table for 10 people and your lunch lasts until 7pm, and no one complains that you're late for your reservation, no one rushes you to leave so the evening diners can have tables, no one brings you the check until you're ready for it, and if you feel like sitting there sucking on your *argileh*[1] and eating *bizr*[2] all night long, the coal will be replaced, the *bizr* will keep coming, and you'll be left in peace to enjoy your *rakhweh*[3]… you might change your tune.

Time is one of the most undervalued commodities in this country. But when it's time to take it easy, no one does it better than we do!

K**s Ikht 7azzeh!

K**s ikht 7azzeh[4] is the number 3 phrase in Lebanon right after *Hallak min shouf*[5] , and in Allah rad[6] . *Iza min shouf*[7] OK, and

---

1 Hookah, water pipe
2 Pumpkin seeds
3 Chillin
4 Damn my luck
5 We'll see
6 If God wills
7 If we see

Allah rad[1] , then when things go wrong, the *7azz* is to blame[2].
Luck!

Tony is driving his brother's M3 the wrong way down a one way street. He knows this but he's being smart and skipping highway traffic. But oops, he forgot one small detail: when you're going the wrong way down a one way street, others have the right of way.

A large truck is driving the right way on said street and suddenly, truck and Tony in Tony's brother's newly painted M3 are level with each other. Truck doesn't care because Truck is bigger, stronger, meaner, leaner, and has the right of way so Truck moves forward.

Tony cares because his brother's M3's new paint job is ending up all over Truck, the beautiful doors are denting inwards, and the scraping screech of metal on metal is causing Tony to piss himself.

Tony gets out of the car, his hair standing to attention on his head, his palms to his cheeks supporting his open mouth in an Edward Munch scream and assesses the damage.

Truck driver gets out and slowly strolls to previously beautiful M3. Truck says: 'This street is one way'. Suddenly the rules count.

Tony says: *'K**s ikht hazzeh!!!* This is my brother's car!'

Plastic Therapy

After cash, plastic is the most valued commodity in Lebanon. Not the recyclable plastic that is (which is too bad since we get through a gazillion plastic water containers each year!).

Plastic is valued to the extent that if you don't have cash, you can get a loan to get some - Plastic surgery - that is!

If you haven't had plastic surgery, you're a nobody. The minimum requirement to join the club is the nose. You have the nose you were born with?! *Quel horreur!*

Another essential: the boobs. Buy one, get the other free, goes the offer.

---

1 God did will
2 (So) If we have seen alright and God has willed, then ...that leaves luck to blame!

Anything below a C-cup requires surgery. How can you live with yourself and a B-cup?! What will the neighbours say?

Other important parts: lips. The all-important Angelina Jolie-pout is what we all need to become attractive, sexy and beautiful. Don't have one yet?! Yalla, quick! Collagen is cheap!

Do you have bony feet?! Well you can't wear open shoes with them like that! Cut the bones out, redo the toes! Who cares if you can never run again! You'll have beautiful feet!

Don't like your eye-brows? Tear them out! Get a tattoo in their place. Ah.... All better!

Your ass is sagging? F**k the gym, get implants.

Slice, dice, chop, fill and redo as often as needed. We're all going to end up looking like *Haifa*[1] anyway, so the sooner it's done, the better!

Just remember that when your kids come out looking nothing like you, when they grow up to be totally insecure about their self-image, when their whole self-worth is measured by what they look like and what size their boobs are, it's cheaper to get them plastic surgery than therapy!

> "F**k the gym, get implants."

---

1 Haifa Wehbe, famous, and infamous, Lebanese star

16_It's Settled

ʃʃʃ

No Escape

When your heart is somewhere, it doesn't matter how hard you try to get away, fate will conspire to bring you back to where you should be. There's just no escape.

I tried Lebanon once before. I came, I saw, but conquer I did not. I ended up leaving despite myself to find work and the intangible happiness we're all looking for.

It turns out though that despite my repeated efforts to leave, the things I value the most are the things that ended up bringing me back home: family, love, culture and country.

'Lashoo rje3teh!'[1] my friends screamed at me.

My reply of 'My boyfriend and family are here! I love being here!' received a disgusted shake of the head.

'Bahleh. Ana ma7allik ma birja3!'[2]

But I tell them it wasn't up to me. It's my Lebanese grandparents' fault. They conspired to bring me home. From the grave they managed to orchestrate my life with skillful dexterity. They filled my mind with memories of us sitting together as one big family on the veranda, sipping coffee and eating fresh figs from the garden trees in a heady fog of jasmine and honeysuckle perfume, memories of helping *Teta* in the kitchen and watching *Jiddo* in the garden… They filled my heart with a ridiculous and indescribable love for Lebanon that has endured with the tenacity of a tick. They filled my soul with a desire to reproduce these memories for my own family in my own country one day, to have kids that speak Arabic and

family, love, culture and country. "

---

1 What did you come back for?!
2 Idiot, In your place (situation), I wouldn't come back!

dance *dabké*[1] and can survive anywhere.

It turns out that my boyfriend's family comes from my *Jiddo's* village, *Douma*. It turns out that my *Teta's* family is distantly related to his *Teta's* family. It turns out that my boyfriend and I have crossed paths unwittingly but repeatedly throughout our lives, *Douma, Keserouan,* Boston, MIT, Nice, and then at a friend's place, just waiting for the right moment for us to actually bump into each other.

I had no choice but to come back: the alternative, to ignore my entire history and myself with a simple one-way ticket.

There was no escape.

Don't you know that you never say 'No' to *Teta* and *Jiddo?!*

Wedding Bells

After 12 years abroad I've come back to Lebanon and, just like the rest of us, this is where I finally find love. After a B.E., an M.S. and PhD, after life on 2 different continents and several cities, I come home for my final degree: my MRS.(!)

Naturally when 2 Lebanese choose to get married, you would expect that they do it Lebanese style.

I've never dreamt about a big traditional Lebanese wedding but I have to admit I thought about it. I thought about it until my best friend started planning hers.

" they ended up inviting 750! "

The planning started a year ahead of time. The wedding was supposed to be small, only three to four hundred people. But the parents had *wejbet*[2] towards other people, and they ended up inviting 750!

The families got into huge arguments because she is from the South and he is from the North. Where to have the wedding?! Each family stubbornly insisted it be in their village. To appease everyone they decided to have the wedding in a church in the South, then drive all the way North for the reception. They would just have to hire transportation for all the guests who wanted to attend both.

---

1 A traditional Arabic folkdance. Each country has its own variation, so that the Lebanese one is distinct from the Iraqi one
2 Obligations

Next came the details. What kind of *zaffeh*[1] did they want, what color and type of flowers, and where to put them, a buffet or a seated dinner, international, French or traditional food menu? Did they want shrimp or salmon? What color place settings? Did they want table covers? Wooden chairs or covered plastic chairs? How to make this wedding more special than any other wedding? Which photographer to pick? Of course they wanted video but how many videographers did they want? The dress, the tuxedos, the pre-dinner drinks, the music, the DJ, the cake… decisions were endless.

All of it could be fun stuff if you like spending a year picking out details for a single day of nuptial bliss, but unfortunately, my friend and her fiancée didn't have very similar tastes and their opinions varied wildly. They got into huge arguments, they yelled at each other, they stopped talking to each other for a few days and then considered breaking up several times.

By the time all was sorted out, both families were frostily polite to each other, the wedding had almost been called off twice, and the whole thing cost only slightly less than the GDP of the country.

On Wedding Day the morning was spent popping valium, chugging champagne, and posing in 1400 different positions for the 3 photographers. By the time the ceremony came around, both bride and groom were numb from medication, and a little tipsy. The reception was a spectacular extravaganza that was over in a few short hours. And just like that, a whole year of preparation, anticipation, trepidation and implementation came to an end with a loud anticlimax. The wedding was over and now they could actually start enjoying each other's company.

The thought of spending a year agonizing over details threw me into panic. I didn't want to waste a year of my life just so I could have a few hours of a really good time. Luckily, my man agreed with me and we headed off to Boston for a civil ceremony. It took a total of one hour to find someone to marry us and reserve a hotel. Five family members showed up, we were dressed and made-up within an hour and strolled to the park along the Charles River. Our wedding officiant met us there under the spring sky and married us quietly to the words of Gibran. Hubby

It took a total of one hour to find someone to marry us and reserve a hotel.

---

1 Entertainment, usually a traditional dance

and I exchanged vows, rings and kisses, took some pictures and then called a cab to our next adventure...

Roots

You've heard a lot from me already about identity issues, who am I, where do I want to live, am I Lebanese or not, if so what kind of Lebanese am I etc. etc. Who doesn't have these issues?! Even Lebanese who have never left home grow up with some sort of identity issue.

I mean look at us! We speak French and English at home instead of Arabic, we have breakfast at Dunkin Donuts and watch MTV, we learn Italian and eat Sushi, we dance Salsa and drink Vodka, we relax at Starbucks and would kill for Brazil during the World Cup, then we go up to the village for the weekend and dance *dabké*. We identify with religion and political parties instead of with our country. We've had every nation from every faith, belief and creed walk across our lands and leave bits of themselves behind for us to absorb. How can we have a solid identity given all this?!

Throw a Lebanese anywhere and they'll land feet first, make a decent living, and still come back home in summer to tell the family about it. We are survivors with a mixed up identity. But I've finally found my footing. I've finally found the little space that I belong to in the world, and am finally comfortable in my skin.

I am Lebanese, I love *kishk*[1] and *mjaddara*[2], and *arak*[3] and *tabbouleh*. I love certain aspects of Lebanon that can't find anywhere else. I was born here, raised here, and Lebanese blood flows through my veins.

I've been to a lot of places and integrated just fine, no problem; I've become an American in the U.S. and gotten Frenchified in France, I spoke Spanish in Spain and ate pasta in Italy. But ultimately though, my history and my roots are

> " Throw a Lebanese anywhere and they'll land feet first "

---

1 As before, cracked wheat and yoghurt mixture fermented into a fine powder (and sometimes taken as a soup or served in bread / on pizza-like dough base as man'ousheh

2 Rice and lentil dish

3 Lebanese anis-flavored liquor, similar to the Greek Ouzo

here in little Lebanon. I had a house in other countries, but when I'm here, I am really 'home'.

I finally know that whether I'm in Lebanon, in Mexico or in South Africa my roots are solidly in Lebanon. It doesn't mean I have to ignore new things I'm learning or new cultures I'm being exposed to. It doesn't mean I need to forget the part of me that's Lebanese either. It just means that I'm a combination of all my experiences; and, although I have roots with the rest of my people here in Lebanon, the tree I grow doesn't have to look the same as theirs, the tree I grow is all mine, different, but still rooted at home...

The lesson is easy but elusive: know where you're from, know who you are, and it doesn't really matter where you're going anymore... you're there already.

The Village Idiot

I feel like such an idiot. I've been to Douma a dozen times already. I've spent an Easter here, attended a wedding lunch and been to the village dinner twice. I've met the same people each time. And they don't forget it!

Hubby keeps reminding me who they are, but somehow there are so many faces all at once that I can't seem to separate and allocate their features to specific persons.

Each time I come up here, someone walks up to hubby and says hello, shakes hands, kisses and hugs him. I stand quietly by his side with a polite smile of 'who-the-f**k-is-this' plastered on my face. Then hubby goes: 'You've met my wife Kathy right?' and they both turn and look at me expectantly.

My smile doesn't budge. Hubby gives no hint of whether I know this person or not. He somehow always forgets that I have a 3 second memory.

> "My smile doesn't budge"

The person reaches their hand out to me to say hello so I blurt out the first thing that I've memorized when meeting people. 'Tsharrafna!'¹' They give me a look of poor-idiot and nod their heads with a half smile.

Hubby shamelessly speaks up at that exact moment. He

---

1 Pleased to meet you!

nudges me with his elbow very obviously and tells me how many times I've met this person before and where.

It's gotten to the point where the entire village thinks I'm an idiot since I keep telling them 'I'm pleased to meet you' over and over again.

Hubby now begs me never to say *tsharrafna* to anyone he introduces me to again. It's getting too embarrassing for him. 'Just say hello and smile, please!' he pleads.

Douma

I woke up this morning to the sound of church bells ringing. We're in Douma and it's Easter Sunday. I crawled out from under the 4 blankets I needed to keep me warm sleeping in the old stone room. The room used to be an old barn, but the stones it's built with are at least a foot thick and trap the cold inside. The wood-run stove went out sometime at midnight.

I wrapped myself in a blanket and walked upstairs and out onto the balcony. The church is just across from us, and I can still see the bell swinging back and forth in the church steeple. It stops ringing just then. The sun pouring in through the *antara*[1] is so deliciously warm that I drop my blanket and just stand in place, like an ice-sculpture melting in the heat. I'm surrounded by gnarled old trees, mountains of green and gray rock, and red tiled roofs. The birds twitter all around, and there is no other sound but the occasional broken muffler of a car built no later than the 1970s, and children's voices somewhere. A TV suddenly starts up and the sing-song of a mass in progress wafts over.

How can I not be happy here? Life is made up of nothing but a series of basic and uncomplicated events. We make food, we eat, we visit people, they visit us, we relax on the balcony in the sun and read, we drink coffee and get into heated political discussions we don't even care about, we go for walks in the surrounding fields, through olive groves and up into flower-filled mountains. That's life here.

I feel like Douma is a little slice of heaven right here on earth;

1 Stone arch

the tranquility is soothing, the tradition is comforting, and the peace I feel when I'm here is so therapeutic it heals my soul. My thoughts turn momentarily to the notion of the new journey of starting my own family and how it would be in Lebanon. can't help but wonder what the future would hold for my kids Would the country be politically stable enough for them to live a secure life or would war chase them away permanently? Would they immerse themselves in the culture and tradition or would they leave and never look back like so many others? Would they grow up to be happy people who love Lebanon and appreciate its defects like we do or would they be indifferent? I hope so for a second before my thoughts drift again.

Last night we had what was called the *hajmi*; a midnight re-enactment of the rising of Christ from the dead. The entire village pours out of their houses and into one of the many churches depending on their religion. Although I'm not any particular religion, we head to the Greek Orthodox Church with hubby's family and friends. We get there early and stand outside for a few minutes. People start to stream into the church square from every alleyway in the vicinity. Old and young, tall and small all dressed in warm winter clothes against the cold night. The air smells of damp night freshness, and the stars above keep calling and winking at us, like they're in on the secret too.

I take a deep breath, look all around me and smile. This was a part of Lebanon that I had never grown up with. I had grown up on the edge of an industrial area where neighbourly gestures were few and far between (unless of course it was to spy on you). Village life: I love it. I love it because I can be a part of it when I want, and I can be a visiting foreigner when I want. The flexibility of transforming yourself as needed is a priceless luxury that is completely acceptable here. *Ajnabiyeh* one day *bint el day3a*[1] (albeit adopted) the other.

Lebanese everywhere are so much more tolerant of you when they know you're foreign or you've lived abroad. They're less likely to hold a grudge, get mad at you for not attending family functions (as in the christening of your sister-in-law's cousin's brother's niece) and for doing things that are 'weird' (like camping out in the woods for two days, or going swimming

> " Village life:
> I love it. "

---

1 Village girl

in December in a wetsuit!).

Right now, I get the best of both worlds, participating in the simple routine of daily life, yet staying far enough away not to get caught up in the gossip of the ladies and the he-said/she-said dramas.

After 12 years of living abroad, I have actually brought some very useful things home with me: understanding, love for my country, open-mindedness, love of nature, compassion, my own identity, and most of all, an enormous appreciation for the amazing riches we have right at home underneath our noses. An appreciation I would never have found had I not been away from *Libnen*, around the world.